ABOUT THIS BOOK

A Japanese kitsune shifter discovers family secrets and hidden truths halfway around the world. She only wanted to find love.

For her more than five hundred years, kitsune Kaori Ishida has never strayed from her beloved homeland of Japan or her family. But when she falls for an American and sees hope of a normal life, she embarks on a journey to the United States. She leaves everything she knows behind, including her familiar appearance, to follow love.

Only, what she finds isn't what she expects.

With the Immigration Act of 1924 only two years old, she discovers a scary new world that doesn't accept either of her true forms. Seeking refuge and following a trail of lies, she ends up in a strange little town in the Colorado mountains, where family secrets and deceptions have her struggling to find the truth—and find herself.

LEGENDS OF HAVENWOOD FALLS BOOKS

Lost in Time by Tish Thawer

Dawn of the Witch Hunters by Morgan Wylie

Redemption's End by Eric R. Asher

Trapped Within a Wish by Brynn Myers

Blood and Damnation by Belinda Boring

Fated Beginnings by E.J. Fechenda

Emeline by Katie M. John

Released From a Curse by Brynn Myers

A Pack of Lies by Kallie Ross

Kiss the Ashes by Desiree Lafawn

Hidden Truths by Colleen Nye

Wrath and Retribution by Belinda Boring

Changing Fate by Char Webster

Rise of the Witch Hunters by Morgan Wylie

The Drowning Bride by Seven Jane

Also try the main Havenwood Falls series; the YA line, Havenwood Falls High; the darker, sexier side of town, Havenwood Falls Sin & Silk; and the local supernatural college, Sun & Moon Academy.

Stay up to date at www.HavenwoodFalls.com

HIDDEN TRUTHS

A LEGENDS OF HAVENWOOD FALLS NOVELLA

COLLEEN NYE

*To all my tabletop, pen & paper, RPG, and virtual gaming friends.
Without you, my knowledge of the supernatural worlds
and beings would be FAR less.*

CHAPTER 1

"This is foolish, Kaori. I simply do not understand." An elderly woman in a kimono held a cup of tea, the lines on her face deep with worry.

"You do not have to understand, *Okaasan*. I'm just grateful for all you've done for me—teaching me more English, helping me get my new clothes, and arranging my passage to the Americas. Not to mention always being home for me in a world I have never felt at home in." Kaori bowed slightly before embracing her mother.

Pulling back and looking over her daughter's expression, Kaori's mother sighed. "It is foolish to travel around the world for a *kareshi*."

"He's more than a boyfriend, *Okaasan*. I plan to marry him. To make him my *shujin*."

Her mother set her tea down and gripped Kaori's hands. "*Watashi no musume*. You are *nobody's* property. Never let anyone be your master."

Kaori chuckled. "I simply meant husband. Even in today's world, in the modern times of the 1920s, we women still want husbands. And he wants me as his wife. I know it. Besides, you know that no matter how much I love our family, I have never felt like I belong."

The older woman nodded slowly. "I know. And I did hear his proposal. But any man who would leave his love to go to the other side of the world, saying goodbye and leaving all that matters behind for money alone, is not honorable."

Kaori's brows furrowed. "*Okaasan*, these are different times than we come from. When will you see this?"

Her mother dropped her hands almost as fast as her expression. "Honor should not have an expiration date in society, *shin'ainaru-kun e.*"

Kaori lifted her hands again. "It's not a matter of honor as much as it is a matter of necessity and laws. Laws of many have changed our world, *Okaasan*. I am not allowed in the States as is. The recent immigration acts prohibit all Asians from entering American soil. Many of our people over there are in camps right now, simply for being of Asian descent. He could not take me with him when his employer wrote for his return because of the risks."

"Then how can you go now?"

"I shall assume a different face and body. We are kitsune. We have this power." Kaori smiled proudly.

"Why didn't you just do this and go with him then? Why wait and travel alone?" Her mother pulled away and lifted the tea once more.

Kaori put a hand on her mother's shoulder. "He does not know what we are. Not yet. But he will, once I explain. I feel it in my soul, *Okaasan*. I need to go."

"Do what you must, but know that I will not rest well without hearing from you. So visit my dreams often. *Kudasai.*" The elder hugged her daughter. "It's been over five hundred years since your birth, and we have never been more than a village away from one another."

"*Okaasan*, you can feel me wherever I am. You can hear the world."

Her mother kissed her forehead. "But I will want to *see* you. Not just spy."

Kaori's eyes filled with tears. "*Watashi wa, anata o aishiteimasu.*"

"I love you, too, Kaori."

Picking up her bags, Kaori gave her mother one last hug, made her way down to the harbor, and boarded the ship to America an Asian woman.

CHAPTER 2

$\mathcal{K}$aori stepped onto American soil in the state of California with the appearance of a slender, attractive, brunette Englishwoman. Her dress was a bit more formal, with the new style slip dress topped with a jacket instead of the commonly seen shawl or stole. She figured, with the exhaustion and stress of the journey, she would need the extra layers to help hide her tails, which liked to slip out when she wasn't keeping them hidden.

Stepping down onto the dock, she pulled out documents from her shoulder bag and presented them as she took in the scenery. Thanks to her contacts in Japan, her paperwork was flawless. However, she worked to say as little as possible, considering that she hadn't had much practice with her accent. As much as she looked of European descent, she wasn't ready to chance anyone's reaction to her having a fluent Japanese accent, despite having just sailed from there.

Refraining from her engrained ritual of bowing when greeting someone, she simply gave a sweet smile. "Hello, sir."

After a brief moment as he looked over her documents, she was granted entrance. "Everything looks good, Miss Ipsley." He handed her back the documents. "Welcome home."

She folded the pages and put them back in her bag. "Katherine or Kay is fine." She tried on her new name.

He tipped his hat. "Have a wonderful day, Miss Ipsley."

"Thank you. You as well." She smiled.

American dollars in hand, Kaori paid a young man on the dock to help her with her trunk and find her a car to a local hotel. It didn't take her even twenty-four hours to plan a route, pay for tickets, and be on her way to Colorado. As eager as she was, she didn't want to waste any time. She boarded a train as early as she could and was on her way to Warren.

∼

"Havenwood Falls, please." Kaori rested her hands on the sill of the ticket window at the train station in Grand Junction, Colorado. "The station in California said they only had tickets for trains to here and to ask once I arrived about getting closer."

The man behind the counter quirked an eyebrow. "I'm sorry, ma'am. Where did you say?"

She cleared her throat and repeated herself. "Havenwood Falls, please."

His brows furrowed at her question. "I'm sorry, miss. I'm not sure we have a train to that town. Is it in Colorado or another state?" He was flipping through a small stack of papers that listed all of the towns the trains went to. "Is it newly established?"

Kaori's heart thudded as her mind raced. She wasn't sure if she'd gotten the name of the town wrong or if she'd purposefully been given the wrong name. Either way, all she knew was that she was standing in a train station in the middle of a foreign country, completely unsure of where to go. Panic rose in her throat, and she fought to keep the guise of her appearance and not to turn into her true fox form and run out of there and all the way back to Japan.

Before she could speak, a tall, dark-haired man stepped up. He loomed over her with his stature, not just in height but build as well. "No trains go up there, but I am going that way, ma'am. You're welcome to ride along." He nodded to the older man behind the counter. "Hello, Fred."

She looked the man over before glancing back at the employee

4

behind the booth, who had moved on to other tasks after nodding in return to being greeted. She was well aware that a human woman should be intimidated or even frightened about going off with some random stranger, especially one his size. It was dangerous even for her. But Kaori wasn't human, and she often had to remind herself of proper reactions to keep up appearances. So she put on a slight show of hesitation. "Alone? Are you um . . ."

He put a hand on her shoulder. "You are safe with me." Dropping his hand, he pulled his coat on. "My name is Theodore Brooks. Or Theo for short. I run a lumber company. I was just dropping my sister off. She was heading home after visiting for holiday."

Adjusting her shoulder bag, she reached a hand out. "Kaor—Katherine. Katherine Ipsley or Kay. Sorry. Either is fine."

He took her hand, much more gently than she expected. "Miss Ipsley, do you have luggage I can assist with?"

Giving up the façade, seeing he wasn't looking for her to be the damsel in distress just so he could pretend to be her knight in shining armor, Kaori motioned to her trunk as she lifted her handbag. "Just this. Thank you."

He gripped the handle and waved his hand for her to go ahead of him. "I'm parked just outside."

The pair stepped out into the brisk Colorado air. Theo opened the passenger door for her before pulling the trunk onto the rear of his truck and securing it with a rope. The entire vehicle jostled as he climbed in behind the wheel, reminding her of his size. But when he gave her a shy smile as he started the engine, she returned the smile and smoothed out her skirts.

After a few twists and turns on the mountain roads and many miles, Theo broke the silence. "Meeting someone?"

"Yes, I am," she replied, staring out over the landscape, still attempting to hide her lack of fluency in the American accent.

"Figures. Nobody comes to Havenwood Falls without a reason." The truck growled as he downshifted. "I won't pry."

She snapped her full attention to him. "I'm so sorry. I didn't mean to be rude."

5

"You're not being rude at all. It is none of my business." Theo pulled the wheel to steer them around a sharp corner.

Kaori took a breath and sat up straight, figuring this was as good a time as any to practice not only speaking but her story as well. "I've been away, and I picked up a bit of an accent, so I am shy about speaking still. Especially with the laws in effect."

"Your accent is barely noticeable." His eyes didn't leave the road.

"Thank you." Her gaze returned to the mountainside. "The gentleman I was planning to marry was called back here sooner than expected, and I am just coming to join him."

He nodded as she spoke. "Oh? In Havenwood Falls? Really? What is his name?"

"Mr. Warren Bennet." She blushed. "He's a bookkeeper."

Sitting upright at Warren's name, Theo's posture became a bit more rigid. He appeared thankful that she was distracted by the view so he could regain his composure. "Ah, yes. Warren. Would you like me to deliver you and your luggage to his home or to your lodgings?"

"You know him?" She turned back, surprised.

"Everyone knows everyone in Havenwood Falls, miss." He turned them around another sharp curve and pulled onto County Road 13.

"Ah yes. I see." She bit her lip. "Since I don't have a room settled as of yet, if you know where he lives, I would love to surprise him. He's not expecting me."

"Oh. No doubt he isn't." Theo chuckled.

"Should I be privy to some information you know that I do not, Mr. Brooks?" Kaori searched his expression, unsettled by his reaction.

He shook his head. "No, ma'am. As I said, this is none of my business. I am just offering you transportation since I was going this way. What you're doing is truly romantic. Such an adventure for a woman."

As much as she wanted to take offense at the comment, he wasn't wrong. The world had made great strides, including the United States allowing women to vote five years prior, but women did not often travel alone, let alone long distances. And women were not likely to do the romantic gesture for a man, especially not one as grand as traveling as far as she had.

Kaori fussed with her hair, repinning a few locks that had fallen astray. "I suppose I'm not a typical woman, Mr. Brooks."

"No, Miss Ipsley. I can see that you are not." She thought she could see a smirk form on his lips for a moment, but it was gone before she could be sure.

"Katherine or Kay, please. We have crossed miles together unchaperoned. I believe we can address each other by our first names." Her words came out more formal than she'd intended.

He matched her tone. "All right. Kay it is, then."

"Thank you." She fought a smile.

Turning the wheel again, Theo drove them through a narrow portion of a side road for a few minutes before turning into a driveway. "Here's Warren's home. Are you sure this is where you want me to leave you? If he's not home, or you decide not to stay, you won't find a car passing by to take you the rest of the way into town."

She peered up the dirt path, thinking for a moment. "No. I'll be fine. He should be home, and he will be overjoyed to see me. I'm sure."

"Well then, Kay, I'll help you unload your trunk. The ground is dry, so you should have no problem wheeling it up to the house. Uninvited and such, I very much doubt Warren would take kindly to seeing you escorted by another man." Theo stopped the vehicle, came around, and held a hand out to her to help her out of the car.

"Thank you." She gave him a slight bow. Quickly, she recovered and attempted to make it a more English bow than Japanese, hoping she didn't look too awkward.

He chuckled. "You know, just because the government doesn't allow Asians in, I'm pretty sure they'll not throw you on a boat, considering you come from here. Besides, how will they see how beautiful a culture it is if they're not exposed to it?"

She moved her hand slowly out of his and looked up at him, slightly surprised. "Have you been there? Asia?"

He nodded. "Yes, ma'am. I did a couple of trips with a shipping line. Not hard for a man like myself to get a job doing grunt work."

She fluffed her skirts out as he unloaded her luggage. "You sound far more educated than what your muscles probably imply for you."

7

A corner of his mouth turned up into a smirk. "Are you implying that I appear uneducated? A ruffian?"

Her eyes went wide. "Oh no! I didn't mean to insult you, sir. I just—"

He stopped her. "I am teasing you, Kay. I understand that my stature lends a certain pre-established sense of who I must be versus who I am. I am older than I look, and I'm far more traveled than most."

She let the tension drop out of her shoulders. "I can relate, Mr. Brooks. Very much so."

He took her hand and kissed the back of it gently. "Theo, please."

"Theo." She smiled and bowed her head.

He returned the gesture. "Good luck, Kay. If you run into any issues with finding accommodations or ever need any lumber while you're here, you know where to find me."

"Yes, I do." She gripped her trunk. "Thank you very much for the escort, Theo. You are very sweet. I hope to see you around town."

"I am sure you will." He climbed back into the vehicle and backed out of the driveway, waving as he pulled out onto the narrow dirt road and out of sight.

Kaori tugged the trunk and started for the house. Her shoulders back, a smile on her face, and her heart racing slightly, she peered through the windows and across the yard to see if she could catch sight of him. But as she closed in on the front porch, she realized that everything was still . . . a bit too still.

Her heart's fluttering turned to pounding as the hairs on the back of her neck stood. Letting her luggage rest on the bottom step, she ascended the rest and stood in front of the door, hand raised to knock but unable to bring herself to do so. Instead, she clasped her hands in front of her, closed her eyes, and breathed.

Waves of her consciousness fanned out, feeling for signs of life. A raccoon, a few mice, and a number of spiders were all inside. A doe and her two offspring were just inside the woods to the east, lapping up water from the creek that ran into the nearby river. And a bear was lazily eating something to the north, a ways into the woods.

There was no sign of a human.

She took a breath and concentrated again, this time searching for less conventional beings. As a kitsune, Kaori had several abilities and heightened senses. And being as old as she was, she had become aware of them. However, she had spent the majority of her life with her family—her mother, father, six brothers, an aunt and uncle, and their eleven kids. Her grandparents had only passed away a little over a hundred years prior. Or, as her kind would see it, they ascended to another level of being, as kitsune do at a thousand years old.

Overall, they were all close-knit and lived in villages together or neighboring villages, moving to new areas when enough time had passed for their extremely decelerated aging to become an issue. Sometimes they joined up with more extended family or even others of their kind. But overall, they strived to fit in and live fairly normal lives. Sure, Kaori and her family were more than aware of their powers and explored them enough to be able to know the basics of what they could do, but they didn't hone them or study them.

So standing there, searching for anyone or anything at Warren's home, she had to work harder at concentrating and focusing on that ability. And when she found nothing, she questioned if she was even doing it right when a voice echoed in her mind. "Remember, Kaori, you will only feel what you're familiar with. Energies you've felt before, whether species or, even stronger, specific beings."

An extremely light sensation of someone she knew mixed with the brief moment of joy she felt, hearing her mother's voice in her head and knowing she was watching over her, was interrupted with a hand on her shoulder. "Kay?"

She spun around, tripping over her own feet, which sent her stumbling into the front door of the house. She let out a small scream caused both by being startled and the fear that she was going to hit the porch. Having to choose between the two, she opted for falling over, keeping her concentration on staying in human form.

She closed her eyes just before feeling a hand grab hers and an arm around her waist. "Woah there. Steady now." He helped her gain her footing. "I didn't mean to frighten you."

A moment later, with her guise in place and breathing controlled, she opened her eyes. "I apologize. I don't normally scare so easily. I hadn't heard you approach."

"Yeah, I left my vehicle by the road in case all was set up here, but I felt bad for leaving you without knowing for sure." Theo took off his bowler hat and dusted it. "If nobody is here, it's quite a distance into town on foot. Not to say you couldn't do it, but I certainly wouldn't want to myself. What kind of gentleman would I be if I allowed a lady such torture?"

Kaori took a step back and pushed away several strands of hair from her face. "You're too kind." She glanced over at the door. "It seems there's nobody here after all. At least not at this time. Maybe it's best if I come into town and find accommodations first. Thank you."

He turned and waved an arm toward the driveway. "Well, then. By all means. Ladies first."

She did a slight bow and walked past him, reaching for her trunk as she stepped down onto the ground.

He walked up next to her and slipped his hand around the handle before she could. "I have this." When she quirked an eyebrow at him, he chuckled. "Again—gentleman."

Together, they made their way to the car and down the road. Once past the almost oppressive woods, they emerged into town. She watched as they passed by houses, buildings, shops, parks, and the occasional person or two walking along the finely manicured sidewalks. A trinket shop, a sign for a restaurant named Napoli's Ristorante Italiano, and City Hall all stood along the sidewalks as proud, American architecture that made the corners of Kaori's mouth curve up as she wondered at the passing scene.

Her eyes opened even wider as they passed Town Square Park. The ornate gazebo adorned the area along with trees, foliage, and pathways. But it was the fountain that caught her eye. As the sun peeked through the clouds, it seemed to almost shimmer in the sunlight in gold tones embedded into the paint. Something about it drew Kaori in, making her follow it with her eyes as they drove on.

"You seem taken with something. I take it Warren is on your mind." Theo stopped at a cross street to let a young couple make their way across.

She blinked. "Warren? Oh. No. I was just taking in our surroundings. I wasn't expecting this."

"This?" he asked.

She had returned her gaze out the window. "Yes. Havenwood Falls is so much more beautiful and progressive than I expected. I think I would like to experience that Italian restaurant soon. It looks very nice." She sounded almost surprised.

He let out a humored scoff. "Did you take us for backwoods and uncivilized?"

Her eyes grew big and cheeks red as she looked over at him. "Oh no, Theo. I didn't mean that. I just . . . I just thought it was a small town in the middle of this huge land. I expected it to be more like one of the many small towns I passed through on my way here. But even you, a lumber company owner, are far from what one would consider a lumberjack. Even your attire is more dapper. And for your size and such, one wouldn't take you for such pleasantries and manners at first sight, I would think. Even your car. A Rolls-Royce Phantom? Not exactly what I would think to see the local lumber yard owners tooling around in. But I'm from Japan—or rather have been there for so long," she tried to correct herself, "that I could be very mistaken."

He patiently listened as she babbled before allowing a grin to form on his lips. "Thank you . . . I think."

Her shoulders dropped. "I'm sorry. I'm coming off all wrong."

Theo steered the car onto the side of the road in front of what looked like a diner. "You know cars?"

She laughed. "Out of all of that, *that* is what you took away from my ramblings?"

He nodded and propped an arm over the back of the seat. "Yes."

She returned the nod. "Yes, I do. I do not know why, but they have fascinated me. Maybe because I always longed to travel more than I have ever been allowed to. A car represents freedom to do so. Beautiful cars like this one"—she ran her hands over the dash—"let you do it in both style and comfort. But—" She paused and studied it for a moment. "This is not the version that the British built. This one was made here in America, no?"

"What makes you say that? The cost of shipping a vehicle like a Rolls-Royce across the ocean?" His eyes searched her face.

She chewed her lip. "No. I believe that wouldn't have been a problem for you. I more say it because of the metals used." She stopped, a bit surprised at her mention of something she shouldn't know about just by looking at the car. "The fuel gauge. It is on the dash. I do not believe that they install those in Britain."

"You are correct." Theo got out and rounded the car, opening her door. "Hungry?"

She eyed him a moment, wondering if he heard her comment about the materials of the car or was ignoring it. "Yes, actually."

Opting to follow his lead on the matter, Kaori gave another slight bow, mentally scolding herself for the gesture.

They took a booth that overlooked the street. She, once again, found herself enraptured by her surroundings. It was so different than her homelands. But there was something even more unusual about Havenwood Falls that seemed to pull her in and fascinate her. It wasn't just the different foods, the difference in the area's vegetation, or even the look of the people and styles of clothing. There was something in the air of the small town that seemed to pull her in.

Her attention was snapped back when the waitress approached the table. "And for you, doll?"

"Excuse me?" She looked up, confused.

The waitress was wearing a bright red shade of lipstick that had left a few specks on her teeth. That would have seemed rather out of place if it wasn't for the woman's obvious preference for too much blush and eyeshadow as well. She sighed. "New to town, I take it?" Before Kaori could reply, she spoke again. "Drink or food? What would you like?"

"Oh!" Kaori glanced at Theo, who was sitting patiently. "Water and soup, please."

"One tall glass of orange juice and the full breakfast for the gentleman and a water and soup for the lady." The server repeated their orders, using a slightly disgusted tone for Kaori's portion.

"I believe you have some teriyaki in the back and maybe some rice? Could you have the cook whip something together with those as well, please?" Theo left his eyes on the woman an extra beat after he spoke.

She didn't reply right away. She just looked at him. Finally, as if she'd stopped breathing for that moment, she took in a sharp breath and smiled. "Sure thing, Mr. Brooks." And she scurried off.

"Meeting you was not accidental, was it?" Kaori sat up straight as she directed her question to Theo.

Taken a bit by surprise, he had to clear his throat before speaking. "Accident?"

Smiling at the waitress as the beverages were set down, Kaori waited until she walked away again before responding. "You being at that train station. There wasn't a sister, and you didn't just happen upon me. It wasn't an accident. You were waiting for *me*, no?"

He opened his mouth to retort, but she continued. "But what I can't figure out is why you came back for me."

Kaori lifted her glass of water, inspected it, then took a long drink, looking over the rim of the glass at him as she did. He hadn't replied. He just sat there, one eyebrow raised and lips slightly pursed. His fingers drummed on the table as she slowly lowered her glass and set it down. "You're smart. And gifted."

"Am I in trouble?"

"Not as much as you probably were."

"Are you in trouble now? And what do you mean by probably?"

The server sat their plates down in front of them, asked if anything else was needed, and left the table again. He leaned back and crossed his arms. "No."

"Ah. There it is." She lifted the first spoonful of soup to her lips and sipped, letting the warmth coat her insides.

He tilted his head. "There what is? And why aren't you trying to run?"

She sipped in another spoonful and dabbed her lips. "Run?" She laughed. "Where would I go? You brought me here down a long, windy road full of dangers. How would I get anywhere? Besides, you came back for me. I'm guessing you know something, and you were delivering me to someone or something, but you changed your mind."

He groaned. "I knew nothing more than I was clearing a debt by picking you up and dropping you off. Nothing more."

"But you had a bad feeling . . . just as I did. Isn't that right, Mr. Brooks?" She set her spoon down.

He sat up. "We're back to last names, Miss Ipsley?"

"You tell me. Should I be fearing for our safety?" She paused. "Theo."

"I don't know."

"No?"

He shook his head. "We will find out soon enough."

"And what about the knowledge of who I am?"

"You mean what you are," he corrected her.

"Tsk tsk." She wagged her finger. "Manners, Theo. I'm a lady, not a beast."

The corner of his mouth turned up. "Consider me corrected. My blunder, my lady."

Her head bowed slightly. "You are forgiven. But yes, you know. Do you not?"

He shook his head. "I know nothing other than I was sent to pick you up. But yes, I can sense something about you."

She studied him for a few moments, taking another sip of her soup without saying anything while trying to work out the situation.

Finally deciding to take a bite of his breakfast, he chewed as she looked at him. "And you? What do you know?"

"I know that I left my country and family to follow my heart. Not just for a man but for my soul. Something pulled me here, and I'm not a foolish, young girl who blindly follows love without something more to it. There was something out at that house I didn't recognize. I also know that you do not vibrate like a mortal. But what I don't know is why I'm here, what you are, and where my Warren is." Worry veiled her expression once again.

After swallowing another bite, Theo sipped his beverage and leaned on the table. "I am going to find out what I can. Like you, I follow my gut when it's yelling at me. And mine told me to come back for you. If I knew anything more, I would tell you."

"Thank you."

"Don't thank me until I make sure I didn't just make matters worse." He noticed she was eyeing the plate of teriyaki chicken. "That is for you. You need to eat. Then we will find you a room at Whisper Falls Inn. I know Mihail and Irina. They own it."

She glanced out the window and back to him, giggling softly. "In a town this size, I'm sure everybody knows everybody."

His teeth gritted together slightly as his hand started rubbing his left wrist. "Speaking of everybody knowing everybody, we will have to make a stop on the way to the inn."

Taking a chunk of the chicken and rice, she nodded toward his arm. "What kind of stop?"

"You have to register." His nostrils flared.

Her eyebrow quirked up. "Register?"

His gazed moved from her to outside the diner. "Yes. They ask that everyone register so they know who all is here and if they're moving in or in town temporarily."

"And if they don't?"

He turned back to her. "Let's just say everyone registers."

"I see." She folded her hands on the table in front of her. "When do I need to do this? On our way to this inn you were telling me about?"

"Yes. Might as well get it done so you can stay long enough to look for Warren." He flagged down the waitress. "Check please."

Kaori worked on the chicken more. "Anything else I should know about this town?"

He chuckled. "So much more."

CHAPTER 3

Standing in the back of City Hall, Kaori glanced between Theo and the plain, utilitarian-looking door. "I'm supposed to trust you enough to go into the back door of a building in some strange town with you?"

He lifted a shoulder as he opened the door. "You got into a vehicle at a strange train station and went to this town with me with less hesitation."

Kaori huffed. "Valid point, Theo."

He reached around her and gripped the handle, pulling it open. She shivered. As she peered into the space inside, her feet refused to move for a moment. She closed her eyes and allowed herself to feel the energies around her. Of course, she felt Theo standing close by, patiently waiting for her to make a move. She also picked up several humans and other beings throughout the building. As far as the level they were entering, it felt mostly empty. That is, until someone appeared inside suddenly, boldly, swiftly moving toward the door. The movements jolted Kaori so much that she stumbled backward.

"Hello," a woman greeted them.

Once again, before she landed on the ground, Theo reached out and steadied her. "Hello, Saundra."

"Good day, Mr. Brooks. Do we have a visitor?" The woman gave a Kaori a smile before looking back at Theo. "She yours?"

"What?" Kaori gasped. "No! I'm spoken for."

"Oh, pardon me." She waved her hand dismissively. "Come in. We will get this over with quickly. I sadly can't visit with you, as I have urgent duties waiting."

Kaori followed as the woman walked back inside. She glanced back to Theo and raised an eyebrow. "What do I need? My documents that I came to this continent with?"

"No." He motioned for her to keep walking. "Your real name, species, and plans while here. They will also ask if you're—"

Saundra interrupted as she sat behind a desk. "Take a seat." Both of them did as instructed. "Name, species, and why you're here. I'll also need to take a blood sample as well as one last thing once we're done . . . if you're granted permission to stay."

"What is that?" Kaori looked back and forth between them.

"Start with your name, species, and why you're here while I take your blood." Saundra stood and rounded the oak desk with the necessary items to take the sample. "Wait. Is there anything I should know about your blood or your skin that would make this difficult or even dangerous?"

Confused, Kaori's eyes went wide as her brows pulled in. "No? I mean, not that I know of."

"Okay, then proceed." Saundra readied the needle.

"Okay?" Still confused, she watched the woman carefully. "My name is Katherine Ipsley."

"Good. Now your real name." Saundra spoke pointedly.

Kaori cleared her throat. "Kaori Ishida."

"Species and reason for coming to Havenwood Falls?" the woman asked.

"I'm a kitsune. And I'm here because I believe the man I was supposed to marry was called back to the States for work, and I've come to be with him." Kaori spoke around the lump in her throat.

Saundra stopped and looked at Kaori. "Kitsune?"

She nodded proudly. "Yes, ma'am."

"Japanese?" Saundra eyed her.

Kaori bowed her head slowly. "Yes."

Theo sat forward, raising a hand. "Kay . . . I mean, Kaori is . . ."

She waved him off. "I am not concerned with the mortal laws. If it was up to most humans, we would all be killed off or sent away. I am curious about her being kitsune. Curious." Saundra looked into Kaori's eyes as if she was studying her. "I believe you are our first."

Kaori attempted a smile. "I hope that my stay is a positive one."

Saundra returned her smile. "I'm sure it will be, as long as we have no troubles. Now, give me a moment. I'll return."

Saundra left with the vial of blood in hand. Kaori inspected the spot where the draw had been taken from, rubbing the bandage that had been taped over it. "What now?"

"We wait," Theo replied.

"For what?"

He sighed. "Approval."

"Then?" She picked at the bandage.

"Your tattoo." Saundra reentered the room with a new set of items in hand.

"Tattoo?" Kaori stood. "I never agreed to a tattoo!"

Saundra stopped and just looked at the woman.

Kaori vigorously shook her head. "No. Is it not illegal?"

"No." Saundra started laying out the items on her desk. "In fact, it's the only way you may legally stay in our town."

Theo leaned up and looked Kaori in the face. "It's okay. In order for you to stay to look for him, you have to register. The tattooing is part of it. But don't worry. It disappears when you leave here. So if you're worried about having it if you return to your family, you can rest assured that won't be an issue."

"It disappears?" she asked.

Saundra nodded. "Yes, it does. Now, I have something to get back to. How about we get this over with?"

After a moment of hesitation, Kaori looked at Theo one more time for reassurance. After he nodded, she held out her arm. "Yes. I need to stay and find Warren."

The needle hit Kaori's arm, and she flinched. Taking a breath, she centered herself as Saundra worked the needle expertly. It didn't take long before it was complete. With a clean cloth, Saundra wiped her skin and put a layer of ointment over it. "There. That will seal it. Just as Theo said, if you leave, this will disappear. Also, if you choose to stay permanently, you *must* come back and register as permanent."

Kaori touched the fresh ink and hissed as it stung. "I will."

Standing, Theo moved toward the door. "Now, the inn. Shall we?"

Seeing he didn't want to stay any longer than necessary, she looked at Saundra. "Are we all set?"

"Yes." She cleaned up and tucked everything away. "Goodbye."

Then she was gone.

Kaori looked around them, confused. "Where did she go?"

Theo shrugged. "I could not tell you. She does that, though."

Her finger traced a circle around her new adornment as the two of them went back out the door and to the car. As he pulled out onto the road, Kaori sighed.

"When I left my village, I thought that with coming to America, I would be the strangest one and would have to hide who I am. But despite being used to living with an entire family of kitsune—my family—I'm encountering even more strange people and things here."

Theo laughed. "You just got here, Kay. Give it time."

"Things get less weird?" she asked.

He shook his head. "No. They get more bizarre."

Another sigh escaped her lungs. "I see."

They drove the rest of the way in silence. Kaori, deep in thought, sat quietly. Obviously struggling with her thoughts, she continued to stay poised in her seat. Just as Theo held his posture as he steered the car in front of the inn.

"Allow me." He got out and rounded the car to open her door.

She exited, giving a slight bow. "Thank you."

After shutting the door, he went back and started to lift the trunk out of the back end of the vehicle, when Kaori screamed.

∽

Theo dropped the trunk. "Kay?"

He ran around, scanning the area.

She was gone, only her attire left in a heap on the ground.

Theo, obviously completely baffled, called out, "Kay? Kay!"

He crossed the front yard of the inn in a few strides, peering around trees, looking for any sign of her. But there was nobody, only a dog that was on a tie near the side of a nearby home. It barked, and Theo realized he'd not registered its bark before that, being used to random neighborhood dogs. Disregarding the dog, he kept looking for anyone. But there was no sign of another person anywhere. And there was no sign of Kaori.

He picked up her gown, shoes, and other garments, laying them in the back seat of his car before setting the jewelry in his pocket, afraid someone might take them. Once everything was secure, he walked in the direction he wouldn't have seen from where he had been standing, continuing to call her name out. "Kay!"

After walking several blocks and crossing the threshold into the woods, he still bellowed for her. His deep voice resonated through the landscape. Pulling back branches and lifting sides of small bushes, Theo sniffed everything, trying to pick up a trail or even a general direction she could have gone. Frustrated, he stopped in a clearing and slowly turned in a circle, examining every tree, bush, and pile of leaves for signs of being disturbed.

He lifted his hands and cupped them, palms facing each other, straight out in front of his chest. Light started to spark between them as he opened his mouth to speak. "Nádar . . ."

He stopped, the sparks in his palm dying out, and he looked down, seeing a fox at his feet. The small creature sat, looking up at him. But when a dog started barking again, the noise echoing into the woods, the fox took off and ran, hiding under a nearby bush.

He walked over and knelt down. "Kay?"

The fox peeked out, sniffing the air.

"The dog?" he asked.

The creature looked him in the eye.

"All right. I'm not sure what to do." He thought for a moment. "I can carry you out and into the car."

She backed up a couple steps.

He chuckled. "Okay. No carrying. I understand. Well? The dog is tied up. If you stay close, I will walk with you and make sure you're in the car before I get in."

She emerged from her hiding spot, trembling softly.

The two made their way back to the vehicle. Theo did just as he said, letting her in first and shutting the door before making his way to his side of the car. The dog was making it well known that it knew they were there. With a hand gripping the handle to his door, Theo gave a low growl and looked back at the animal. The dog, tail between his legs, bowed down to the ground and stopped its noisemaking.

He got in, started the car, and pulled away. Kaori, still in fox form, sat in the passenger seat, curled up in her tail, trembling.

Once around the corner, Theo glanced over at her. "I take it you will need your clothes and a private place to put them on in order to return to human form. There's a limited number of places I can take you, so I will just take you to my home. I have a spare bedroom that my sister uses when she is visiting. Nobody will bother you there."

Theo drove up his driveway and parked, letting Kaori out and leading her inside. He showed her to the spare room and set her garments and jewelry on the bed, closing the door tight behind him.

Several minutes later, Kaori emerged into the living room, fastened neatly into her dress, her hair pulled up just as it had been before her transition. Her cheeks were red, and her head was tilted down. "My apologies. I do not do well around dogs."

Theo laughed, doubling over slightly. "That is perfect."

"Perfect?" Kaori was confused.

He gathered himself. "It is my turn to apologize. It's just . . . well? You're a shifter, no?"

"I am kitsune," she replied.

"Kistune?"

She nodded. "Yes, I am fox. But we can transform into humans or even other creatures. The older we are, the more abilities we have and the stronger we are." She shifted her appearance into her Japanese human form. "This is what I am used to looking like as a human . . . you already saw me as a fox." She blushed again.

"Very interested. I would love to learn more," he said.

She bowed. "For helping me, I would love to tell you more. But I'm curious what species you are. I can sense you are not human. And I know it by the registration process and knowledge." She held up her freshly tattooed wrist.

He pushed the sleeve of his right arm up, revealing one of his own. "I am not human. I am . . . complicated."

"Complicated? Do explain." She took a seat.

He pursed his lips, thinking over his words. "To start, I am druid. My mother's family lineage is druid. We believe and practice what many see as magic."

"Not unlike those we call Shinto," she observed.

"Yes," he agreed. "But that is not all. I am also lycan."

She tilted her head.

"My father's lineage is lycan. So, I am a shifter like you. There are shifters and were-kin in the world, yes. Lycan are a bit different, though. I shift into a wolf—larger than normal wolves by far, and I'm forced to shift on the full moon. But I'm capable of shifting other times as well. And I also shift into a bipedal form. I suppose, really, it's simpler to say we have more than one form of wolf, which makes me different than other wolf shifters. But . . ."

She sat up. "This is why you were laughing. You're a dog."

He crossed his arms. "I am lycan. Thus, wolf, not dog. But I am part canine. Yes."

Kaori watched him, her eyes studying him as neither spoke. Occasionally, her eyebrows would pull in, then release. A smile would sneak onto her lips, then disappear. Finally, she let out a sigh and bit her lip. "I do not seem to fear you like I do other dogs."

"Wolf—canine. Not dog," he corrected her.

She shrugged. "Large dog-wolf person with magical powers. I have no room to judge you. I am a fox that is able to appear human and has magical powers as well. We are not unalike in that matter."

He chuckled. "You have a very valid point, Kay." He held his hand out to her. "Allies then?"

She shook his hand. "Yes. That is most appreciated."

"Now, we need to figure out accommodations for you. Then we can sort out this Warren situation." Theo wrung his hands.

"Yes. A place to stay would be very good, but . . ." Kaori glanced off in the direction of the dog. "How many dogs are in town? Are they all tied up or roaming free? How often is that one, out there, able to be out?" She rapid-fired off question after question.

He studied her for a moment. "Your fear is strong, isn't it?"

She brought her gaze back to him. "Yes." She shook her head as if trying to clear it. "Not unlike the legendary strife between vampires and werewolves, kitsune fear dogs. It's almost ingrained in us. Like a child fearing the dark or their bedroom closet at night."

"Or my fear of clowns. I don't know why and can't explain it, but clowns freak me out." Theo chuckled nervously.

She nodded, her eyes not leaving his face. "That's a pretty strange fear, Theo."

"Yes. I suppose it makes far less sense than your fear of dogs." Theo shrugged, shifting his weight between his feet. "I gather staying at the inn is going to be a problem with the dog across the street. Therefore, I propose you stay in my spare bedroom. My sister will not be back in Havenwood Falls for a while, so it will just be sitting empty."

"I wouldn't dream of imposing on you." Kaori clasped her hands.

He stepped to the hallway and pulled a quilt out of the linen closet there. "You would not be a bother. The company would be nice. Plus, then I will be easier to get in touch with should you need someone."

"But—"

"But nothing." He handed her the quilt. "I cannot, in good conscience, allow you to not have a place to stay. Now, bring the quilt, and we can change the dusty bed coverings with clean ones. Then I will retrieve your trunk for you." He saw the worried look on her face. "Unless you truly oppose. I wouldn't want to force you into a situation you were entirely uncomfortable with."

The decision not only weighed on her mind but showed in her features as well. Still wringing her hands, she took a couple breaths before replying. "It is not customary. Some may even say it is inappropriate. However, I cannot bear the idea of going near that mongrel by the inn every day. So if you say there is no other inn, then I must accept your offer. And if you do not mind, I would like to cook dinner if you could just take me to a market to purchase a few supplies."

"I am glad to hear it. I will retrieve your things from the car. There is a private bathroom off your bedroom. Make yourself comfortable. You are welcome to go to the kitchen and see what I have. If you do not find what you need, we can go to the market then."

Kaori bowed. "You are most generous. I am thankful for you."

"It is no problem at all. I will return." He left to get her trunk.

Once settled, Kaori surveyed the contents of the kitchen before joining Theo in the living room. He was sitting and reading a book by candlelight, the rocking chair he sat in creaking with the occasional shift of his weight.

She stood in the archway that separated the living room from the kitchen, debating whether to offer to turn on the lamp but figuring his lighting choice was a preference. "Have you not had a woman in this home for a while?"

"A woman?" he asked, puzzled.

"Yes." She giggled. "I believe all I found was meat and potatoes. I did not even find a cellar filled with jars of food."

"It seems my sister's absence has taken a toll on my menu. Then I say we should go into town and pick up something other than meat and potatoes." He smirked.

"Yes, we should," she agreed.

It was a short drive there, just as most things were in such a small town. Granted, to get to the nearest city or anything else, it would take a stretch of time. But within the town itself? Kaori marveled once again as they drove, taking in the shop signs, architecture, and the people. Only this time, it was as if a veil had been taken off her eyes; she finally let her kitsune senses kick in and felt the essence of those around her. It was something she normally blocked. This time, though, she allowed herself to open up. She knew that many, if not most, of those people were not humans. And this made her wonder what species they each were. Her expression conveyed her fascination as her eyes darted around.

"I am surprised at your excitement. You have spent your life in a large family of supernatural beings. Yet you seem in awe of the cluster of them here." Theo turned off the engine in front of the general store.

"Oh!" Kaori spun in her seat. "I am only used to my kind—kitsune. I have come across some others. At my age, I am not entirely sheltered. Yet, never in a setting such as this. So many in one place . . . all living together in harmony, it seems."

"Havenwood Falls is definitely a unique town. But it is not without some struggle that we achieve this." He opened his door. "I will be right around."

She exited as he opened her door. "Thank you."

Inside, Theo made his way to the counter. "Good day, Laura. How is business?"

A petite woman set a couple of packaged items on a shelf behind the counter and turned around. "Good. It pays to be the only store in a town that carries basic necessities."

He chuckled. "That's very true."

She grinned. "Not unlike being the lumber yard owner, no?"

"Exactly." He glanced over at Kaori, who was gathering items off a list she'd made. "Hey, I was wondering—you see people coming in and out of here all the time. And I suppose many people stop and fill you in on things as they pass through."

"Not unlike being a bartender some days," she agreed.

He leaned against the counter casually, turned slightly away to be able to see Kaori. "You wouldn't happen to know a Warren Bennet, would you? He'd be new to town, if he's here."

She thought for a moment, straightening the stack of packaged cigarettes near her as she did. "No, not that I can think of. But there are people that come through town all the time. That Porter Patterson that lives up on the mountainside always has people in and out of his place, and sometimes they come down here to purchase goods."

"Porter, huh?" He pulled his wallet out as Kaori approached.

"Yes." Laura started pushing buttons on her metal cash register, totaling up the items Kaori had selected and placing them in paper bags. She gave Theo an inquisitive look. "And who is this?"

"My apologies, ladies." He stood up straight. "Laura, this is Kay.

She just arrived and is here looking for Warren, her fiancé. Kay, this is Laura. She owns and runs this shop. A mighty fine achievement for a woman, if you ask me."

Laura smirked. "When the previous owner passed, the store was going to close. I saw a need, and I provided it. It is not as if this town is conventional. Thus, I was able to take over the general store without too much strife from the menfolk."

Kaori held a hand out. "It is very nice to meet you. Congratulations on your success."

Laura returned the gesture and finished bagging the several items Theo and Kay had brought to the counter. "Thank you. Two dollars and sixteen cents, please."

Kaori started to open her purse. "Yes. Of course."

But Theo beat her to it. "Here you go. Keep the change. Let me know if you find anything out, if you don't mind?"

Laura took the money from him and slipped it into the drawer. "Will do."

"It was very nice to meet you." Kaori went for the bags.

Again, Theo beat her to it. "See you soon."

With a slight twinkle in her eyes, she replied to him, "I certainly hope so."

Once back in the car, Kaori giggled. "She likes you very much."

"Yes. We are good friends. I have helped her with most of the shelving and a number of other things for her store," he explained.

"No," she argued. "She likes you for more than a handyman."

He blinked. "You think?"

"I know," she replied.

He laughed. "You *know*? One of your gifts?"

She pursed her lips. "Simple observation reveals that, but I do have a couple of other gifts that aided me in this conclusion. Have you considered her in that way?"

He cleared his throat. "No, not that I can think of. She has always just been my friend."

"I see," Kaori said.

The matter was dropped. While they drove back through town, Kaori's enthusiasm was far less as she watched out the window. Her hands were folded in her lap, the corners of her mouth turned down, and her shoulders set and poised. Seeing her change in demeanor, Theo asked, "Would you like to drive by the house one more time and see if there's a car or a buggy?"

She perked up. "As wonderful as that would be, I do not want to inconvenience you any more than I already am."

"Nonsense." He waved a hand. "You are no bother. This town can be downright sleepy at times. And as much as I prefer things that way, I do not mind helping someone in need. I would just be home reading today, otherwise. Instead, I will be getting a home-cooked meal other than meat and potatoes."

She giggled. "Then I shall find something more to do in exchange for your kindness." Her eyes returned to the scenery, a little brighter again. "Thank you."

"You are very welcome."

Taking County Road 13 back out of town, Theo drove into the driveway this time, pulling up to the house. "I'll get out and look around. I'll be right back."

Kaori waited several minutes, but when he didn't come back around the house, she started to climb out, worried.

"Theo?" she called out. "Is everything okay?"

Silence greeted her for only a moment before he came jogging around from behind the house, slightly out of breath. "I checked back in the woods a ways to see if maybe he was gathering firewood or anything. I hope I didn't alarm you."

"I suppose I am on edge, that is all," she replied. "I did not mean to overreact."

He crossed the yard and opened her door for her. "Kaori, I would not have blamed you if you had run across the yard crying. You've been through enough."

"I've been through far worse in my years," she exclaimed once back in the car.

"*That* I do not doubt."

CHAPTER 4

*T*heo had asked Kaori several times if she would like or need help in the kitchen, but she insisted she was fine. Finally, she asked for several sticks—"thin as twigs but sturdy as branches"—for her to finish cooking the dish she was working on. He retrieved them, then brought in some firewood and went to his chair. He had taken up residence back in his rocking chair, reading a book.

Once dinner was ready, she called him in to the table, where he found a spread of yakitori, rice, and a pot of udon noodle soup. He took his seat, and she dished out a serving as he took a deep breath, smelling the aromas. "This smells delicious."

"Arigatu." She bowed slightly. "I will have to learn more recipes from other cultures. And maybe Laura can procure some foods that I could use for more of my people's dishes, as well."

After waiting for her to sit with a full plate and bowl as well, he took his first bite. "If this is the quality of meals you'll keep cooking while you're here, I will certainly make sure she does, or I will go into the city myself."

A blush washed over Kaori's cheeks. "You are too kind."

He tapped the corners of his mouth with a napkin. "Laura can usually find anything I ask her for. Which reminds me. Since she is privy to a lot of the town's chattering, I asked her if she had seen your Warren."

"You did?" She perked up with a child's enthusiasm. "Has he been in there recently? Does she know where I might find him?"

He shook his head solemnly. "No. I'm so sorry. She has not seen him nor heard of his whereabouts."

"So we're no closer to knowing anything." Kaori looked defeated.

"I'm truly sorry, Kay. But this could be as simple as him having gone into the city for supplies or being at work. You told me he came back for his job."

"He did." She set her napkin on the table. "He would have made it here three weeks ago. The fact that we cannot find him has stirred something in my stomach that's sour."

"Supplies. Like I said, I think he's just gone for supplies." Theo sat up straight, confident in his statement.

"I am sure I am just anxious to see him. You are probably right." She laid her napkin back across her lap and finished her meal in silence.

Theo didn't disturb her, seeing she obviously needed a moment to let her thoughts process. When they were done, he insisted on clearing the table and washing the dishes himself. "You go rest. The journey here surely must have taken a toll on you. Take a nap, read a book, whatever you need to rest. If you need to go outside, though, please let me know. You shouldn't be out there on your own, being new to town. You do not know what is in the woods yet, and they do not know you."

She gave a weak smile. "A book sounds fine just about now." She was crossing the threshold into the living room when she turned around. "Thank you, Theo. Very much."

He tipped his head. "Just rest. You will see him soon enough."

"I hope so." Kaori handed him the last dish off the table and went into the spare room, closing the door behind her.

～

Kaori emerged from the room after falling asleep while reading, not sure how much time had passed. She walked through the common areas of the house to find Theo and let him know she was up, but she did not find him. Thinking he possibly went into his own room for a nap himself, she went out onto the front porch to sit.

A few moments later, the silence was interrupted by the sound of Theo's voice. "No. I need to know if he's even here, or if I'm just participating in some wild goose chase. For that matter, if he even exists at all. That woman is starting to panic."

A woman's voice replied. "As you were told, you know only what you need to know. You were supposed to drop her off and then wash your hands of it."

"I owed Porter one favor. And that favor was to pick her up, pretend to know Warren and where he lived, and bring her to Havenwood Falls. I fulfilled this." His tone was growing more tense as he spoke.

She replied with equal frustration. "You were supposed to leave her at that house for us."

"For what?" His words were pointed.

She didn't pause. "*That* is none of your concern, Theodore."

A wind picked up, making it hard to hear what was said next, but when it died down, she heard him say, "It is my issue when I was the one to bring her here. Now explain to me what is going on."

"I cannot," the woman replied.

"Then she stays with me until she gives up on this Warren or decides to go home. I do not trust Porter or anyone who works for him."

The woman growled. "Yet you agreed to bring her here for him?"

"I made the mistake of getting into debt with him on a job . . . a small debt. A mistake I will never make again. And I fulfilled that. But I could not, in good conscience, leave that lady to lord knows what he had planned for her." The winds picked up for another quick moment.

"That's where you're wrong. Porter wants me to bring her to him. So I will be taking her with me." There was a snarky confidence in the woman's voice.

Kaori heard crunching as if someone's footfalls were heavy. "I would like to see you try to take her. But I must advise against it."

Both the heavy footfalls and another set started coming around the side of the house. Holding her breath, Kaori tucked herself back inside the door and readied herself to transform, if needed. She pressed her back against the wall just inside the door, but only one set of feet came across the snow and up the porch steps.

Slowly, she turned and dared to peek through the sheer curtain that adorned the front window. Theo was standing, facing the direction of the driveway, arms crossed over his chest, shoulders tight. She could see them rise and fall with every slow, deliberate breath he took.

She carefully opened the door and stepped out onto the porch. "I am in some trouble, am I not?"

"Get back inside. It is not safe for you outside right now." He took her by the arm, a bit more gently than she expected, and guided her back inside.

"I am not wrong."

"You overheard?"

She looked down at her clasped hands. "Yes."

He looked at her solemnly. "No. You are not wrong."

She took a deep breath. "Warren . . . is he . . ."

"I do not know." He dropped his hands. "These people cannot be trusted. I do not know who that woman is . . . or *what* she is. But Porter Patterson is not a good man. What he wants with you cannot be a good thing, knowing your abilities."

"But what if they have Warren?" Panic filled her eyes with tears.

"I will do what I can to find out, but this man . . . he lives in a large home in the woods. I'd say he's secluded out there, but he has people coming and going day and night. Trust me, none of it is good dealings. He owns a portion of the railroad, which makes him rich. And he did not attain it, nor his riches, by honorable means." Theo stepped inside, closing the door and bolting it. "I am not sure anyone in town has much to do with him. And those that do are either in trouble from their ties to him or just as bad as he is."

She slumped down onto the window bench, the tears that were

filling her eyes moments before now sliding down her cheeks. "I do not want to put you in danger."

"What do you mean?" He knelt down in front of her.

Her eyes were ringed with red. "My being here puts you in danger. Like you said, you do not know who or what that woman was. She could have harmed you." Kaori stood, adjusting her dress. "I cannot put you in any more danger. I will just find this Porter Patterson's house, sneak there in my fox form, and see if I can find Warren myself."

"Kay, that is not safe."

"Neither is me being here. For you . . . for either of us."

"I can handle them."

She paced. "I cannot."

"And I cannot let you walk into danger alone."

They stopped and looked at each other, both standing with postures that betrayed something beyond their stubbornness. Both obviously concerned and unwilling to walk away.

Kaori broke the standoff first. "Why?"

"Why what?" he asked.

She huffed. "Why are you deliberately putting yourself in danger for some strange woman?"

"Why are you so willing to put yourself in unknown danger when someone is willing to help you?"

She crossed her arms. "Do not answer my question with a question."

"Fine." He mirrored her stance. "I do not know."

"You . . . what?" She scrunched her face. "You do not know?"

He relaxed his stance. "No. Could be because I have too big a heart to let someone get hurt when I'm sure that is what will happen. Could be my protective nature. Could be that there is something about you. Could be . . ."

She stormed out of the room.

Left standing in the middle of the living room, Theo growled deep and low. "Could be because I'm a fool."

Kaori did not come out of the spare room the rest of the night.

CHAPTER 5

The aromas of bacon, eggs, flapjacks, and potatoes filled the air. Various shades of reds, yellows, and oranges had invaded the dark blues of the early morning sky, overpowering the twinkling white light of the stars. Theo stood at the stove, flipping a golden brown flapjack while munching on a slice of crisp bacon. His eyelids were drooping as his mouth opened wide in a yawn.

"Good morning." Kaori's voice was soft.

He turned and saw her standing in the archway. "Good morning. I hope you are hungry."

"I have never had an American-style breakfast before." She didn't move from her position.

Tossing the flapjack onto a plate, he shoveled on some of each of the other foods that were prepared and set it on the table. "There's fresh-squeezed orange juice in the icebox. Help yourself."

"I couldn't—" she started.

He whipped around, spatula in hand. "Sit. Eat. Enjoy some orange juice. And relax. For someone from your culture, you are awfully uptight."

"I just don't want to keep putting you out." She made her way to the end of the table and placed her hands on the edge.

He poured more batter into the cast-iron skillet. "You'd be putting me through worse by not letting me help at this point."

She eyed him, studying his posture as much as his words. "I can see that now. My apologies."

He stomped over to the icebox, yanked out the canister of orange juice, and dropped it onto the table next to two juice glasses. "And if you wouldn't mind, please stop apologizing."

"I'm s—" She rolled her lips in between her teeth. "Yes. I will do my best."

"Good." He went back to the stovetop just in time to flip the contents of each of the pans before anything burned.

Together, they ate, neither saying much more than how delicious the food was and what Theo had to do down at the lumberyard that day. He insisted Kaori come with him, since leaving her alone in his home left her vulnerable.

She was reluctant, but seeing he was firm, she gave in. "Maybe I can be of some help to repay you."

"I am sure I can find something for you to do. I can understand the need to feel of some use." He started clearing the dishes.

She took them from him. "You cleaned when I cooked. I will do the same for you before I get ready."

"Deal." He smiled.

She made quick work of cleaning up the kitchen and herself, emerging from the room in a fresh knit dress, her hair pinned up stylishly, with a modest amount of makeup on. "I hope I did not delay you."

"No." He stood from his rocking chair. "This allowed me to get some reading in that I didn't accomplish last night."

"Good." She fought a smile.

"Yes. Good."

The tension between them was thick. And it continued. The drive was silent other than the noise of the car and the sounds of nature around them. Once again, Kaori found herself gazing out the window as they drove the several miles to Brooks Lumber.

Theo held the door open for her and introduced several employees to Kaori, being careful to refer to her as Kay, on their way into the office. They stopped at the front counter, which was situated in front of his office. He waved his hand toward the woman behind the register. "This is Winnifred Rose. She runs our front counter and tends to keep many of the boys in line around here."

"Including you, Mr. Brooks," she added with a giggle.

"Including me at times, yes, Winnie." He chuckled. "This is Kay. She is a friend from out of town . . . and recently out of the country. She will probably be helping me out with some office work here and there while she is in Havenwood Falls."

Winnie looked Kaori up and down before fixing a polite smile on her face. "Nice to meet you."

"Nice to meet you, too," Kaori replied.

But before her words were fully out, Winnie had gone back to her paperwork, glancing up only once more with a not-so-pleased expression on her face.

Once in the office with the door closed, Kaori laughed. "You certainly have a trail of weeping women around here."

He was shuffling through some paperwork. "Excuse me?"

"You cannot possibly pretend to be oblivious that the woman you employ out there is completely taken with you." Kaori sat, crossing her legs and smirking.

He looked up, puzzlement pulling his eyebrows together. "I umm . . . well? I suppose I never thought much about it, let alone took any notice. But you certainly take quite a lot of notice of my love life."

"I just . . . I didn't mean to . . ." She stumbled over her words.

He roared with laughter. "I am teasing you, Kay."

She scrunched her nose. "Funny."

"Yes, I can be from time to time." He continued to laugh as he pulled a box out from under some pages. "Here. I need to go out into the yard and check on my crews. This box is all of the paid invoices that need to be checked against the receipts and totaled by month in the enclosed ledger." He then pointed out other boxes, explaining what needed to be done with those as well.

Kaori took the first box and set it on her lap. "I will do my best."

She looked around at the cluttered and dusty room, filled with haphazard stacks of file boxes, paperwork, samples, and so much more.

He grinned. "I have no doubt."

He looked nervous, hovering a bit longer than needed over the desk.

She stayed sitting as he made his way to the door slowly, her hands over the box he had handed her. "I will stay in here."

"Yes, that will be good. I will try to check on you, but I need to push my guys, get them on task, and get it done with as quickly as possible so we can just leave." He gripped the doorknob. "If you need anything, feel free to ask Winnie. She can get you what you need."

"I doubt she will enjoy waiting on me." A corner of her mouth turned up.

He blinked, a slight blush on his cheeks. "Yeah, well, she can set that aside. I'll be back." He ducked out of the room, shutting the door behind him.

Kaori heard Theo on the other side of the wall instructing Winnie to take care of anything Kaori might need, still being careful to call her Kay instead of her real name. The other side of her mouth turned up, joining the one side and making a full smile. A smile that Kaori quashed once she felt it hit her eyes.

"Work. You are here to work to repay this man for helping. Nothing more." She stalked over to the desk and started in on the invoices.

She was so engrossed in her work that she barely looked up and hadn't noticed he hadn't peeked his head in for a few hours. But when he did, his jaw dropped. "Wow. What did you do?"

She blew at a strand of hair that had come loose and was hanging in front of her face, tickling her nose. "I'm sorry. Did I do something wrong?"

He cleared his throat. "What did I say about apologizing?"

"To stop."

"Exactly."

"So I did not do something wrong?"

"I am not sure yet." His eyes were wide. "Would you care to explain where all of my paperwork, boxes, and ledgers are?"

"Yes." She stood from the office chair. "I finished all of the invoices, then moved on to sorting the rest of the paperwork, making sure to set them in their appropriate boxes once I found the others in the cabinets. There was a young man that came looking for you, and he knew where you kept a number of empty file boxes, and he retrieved several more for me. I wrote labels out for each, and they are put away by chronological order and organized. I hope it is a system that makes sense for you. And all the samples are in their own bin over by the door for quick access if a customer needs to view them. Everything has its place now." She gasped. "Oh. Except these. I was unsure what to do with these." She handed him a small stack of invoices.

He took them on his way to the wall of cabinets. Looking in, he found all of the boxes labeled, stacked, and neater than he'd ever had his office. The current ledgers were on his desk in a stack. The top of his desk was cleaned and organized. And there were no more piles of anything on the floor. He finally looked at the pages she'd handed him. "Oh wow. Yeah. These are long-unpaid accounts. I might as well give up on them."

She took them back. "We will see about that."

He took them back from her and tossed them onto the desk. "How about we retire for the day. Since you did a year's worth of work today, you can focus on that next time."

She glanced over at the small stack. "Okay."

"Shall we?" He motioned for the door.

"Okay." She followed him, reaching over and straightening the stack on her way past.

He chuckled as he held the door and let her pass.

"Have a good rest of your day, Winnie." He nodded at the woman as they walked by her.

She had caught a glimpse past the door in his office and shot Kaori a glance, ignoring her in her response. "See you soon, Theodore."

The level of obvious flirting was almost as embarrassing as the amount of cleavage she showed. Kaori, diverting her eyes, fought her nose from curling in disgust. Instead, she gathered her composure and gave the woman a sweet smile. "It was *very* nice meeting you. I am sure I will see you around often."

Winnie huffed. "Goodbye."

A snarky grin played on Kaori's lips as she left with Theo.

"You're a lot more feisty than I took you for." Theo closed her car door and went around, getting behind the wheel.

"Oh?" She sat, poised, her hands in her lap.

He scoffed, amused. "It works for you."

Winnie was standing inside, looking out the large picture window on the front of the showroom. The lettering for "Brooks Lumber" curved in gold, almost hiding her face and her failed attempt to appear as if she wasn't looking out at them.

Kaori plastered on a cheesy grin and waved. "She seems nice."

Theo shook his head. "Not looking to make friends, are you?"

Folding her hands in her lap once more, she lifted a shoulder. "Friends? Yes. You are my friend. She would never be a true friend."

"I cannot argue with you on that point. She has few friends." The rocks crunched under the tires as they pulled away from the building.

"Do you?" she asked. "Have friends, that is. Do you have friends?"

"What?" He blinked.

She giggled. "Do you have friends?"

"Is that supposed to be a sincere question or a mocking stab at me?" His eyes stayed on the road.

She shrugged. "You know? I'm not sure. Maybe both?"

They both looked at each other, paused, then began to laugh.

Conversation continued, both of them relating stories of people they'd known with similar temperaments. The whole ride, Kaori continued to tease Theo about Winnie's obvious affections for him. He continued to deny it, which just encouraged her all that much more.

The rest of the day was relatively calm as the two of them cleaned, ate, read, and chatted. Whatever nervousness Kaori was holding onto, as far as staying with Theo went, disappeared with the level of comfort they had with each other. At one point, she brought up her predicament, but she calmed with his confidence as he explained he would start making further inquiries first thing in the morning.

Later that night, when Kaori couldn't sleep, she knew it was far less her accommodations and precisely her concern for Warren and unease about her situation. Her mind was racing. Unable to just continue to lie there, Kaori got up, pulled on a sweater and shoes, and made her way out into the backyard.

There was a slight chill in the air for an early summer night, but the sky was clear, the moon was bright, and Kaori was feeling like her shoulders were not so burdened. She stepped down onto the grass and breathed in deep. Her hands ran across the leaves of a nearby bush as she left the bottom step and ventured out into the yard.

The landscape being so different than her home back in Japan, Kaori marveled at her surroundings. And for the first time, she did it do not through a vehicle window but standing on the ground, still. She was able to feel the breeze tickle her cheeks, the brush of the greenery on her palms, the prick of the twigs on her flesh.

The light from the moon lit up the yard, illuminating the lush foliage where she'd wandered to the edge of the woods that bordered the manicured lawn. Hearing some rustling in front of her, she let her eyes focus and saw a large raccoon and her babies emerging from the pile of leaves beneath the large oak tree she was standing under. She knelt down and reached out, allowing the raccoon to sniff her fingers before the animal scurried away, nudging her babies along with her.

Kaori stood back up and took in her surroundings. Contentment played across her features, and, for the first time in a long time, she felt at peace.

Theo woke, his arms stretching out over his head as a yawn escaped him. It had been such a long time since he'd had a pleasant night relaxing and conversing with someone. Something about the interaction was calming. So calming that it also seemed to have brought about the first good night's sleep he'd had in even longer.

He flung the comforter off, slipped his feet into his slippers, and pulled on his robe before emerging from his room. Checking the time on the grandfather clock in the living room, he was a little surprised that Kaori wasn't up. Chalking it up to her possibly having an equally good night's sleep, he decided to make breakfast again. After all, his stomach was grumbling and growing louder.

Opting for omelets and toast, he scrambled up the eggs, cut a slab of ham into chunks, and diced the onion and tomato. While everything was cooking, he shredded some cheese and started grilling the bread over the fire. Finally, as he plated everything, he checked the icebox to make sure there was some fresh orange juice left, enough for both of them.

Satisfied, he knocked on the door to the spare room. "Kay, I made breakfast. Care to join me?" He didn't hear a response, so he knocked again. "Kay? Are you feeling unwell?"

A slight rustling sound came from the other side of the door but no reply.

Waiting a moment, a little bit of his excitement for the day washed away as he took a step back from the door. "I hope you slept well. Your plate is on the table if you are hungry."

He waited one more moment before turning away and going back to the kitchen. He sat and ate his breakfast. Eating alone had never been an issue for him before, but something about it that morning was different. Something about it felt a bit empty.

He picked up his plate, took it to the sink, and set it down a little harder than intended. Theo gripped the side of the sink, nostrils flaring as he huffed at his own foolishness. "She is spoken for, you fool. A friend and nothing more."

Gruffly, he washed the morning dishes, putting her still full plate of food in the icebox in case she emerged hungry later on. Not quite feeling settled, he went outside and chopped some wood, took a bath, then straightened the already spotless living room. Still, something was unsettling him.

Realizing he hadn't seen Kaori all morning, he knocked on the door once again. "Kay? I'm a bit concerned about you."

He waited for just a moment before turning the doorknob. "I'm coming in."

Slowly, he pushed the door open. Leaning in, he looked around. "Kay?"

He stepped across the threshold.

Nobody answered, and nobody was in the room. He checked and found her trunk, its contents and several of her belongings still in place. The bed was made. Her handbag was on the stand next to the armoire. All signs pointed to the fact she was there, but he did not see her.

Wondering if they'd simply not crossed paths as he moved about the house, he went back out and searched through the other rooms. Emerging out the back door, finishing with the kitchen last, Theo stood on the back deck and sniffed the air, trying to pick up any scent of her, his nose twitching.

He jumped as footfalls sounded up the side steps to the wood platform. Relieved, he sighed. "Kay. Thank goodness."

She was smiling from ear to ear. "Theo! I have fantastic news!"

His words came with a growl. "Where have you been? You had me worried half to death!"

She batted her eyes. "I'm sorry. I didn't mean to."

"Please stop doing that to me." He relaxed his shoulders. "Now, what is this fantastic news?"

She clapped her hands in front of her. "Warren! He is here! Well, not here, but he is in town! I was able to see him this morning, and he has asked me to join him as he leaves for New York with his company. I am leaving with him, Theodore. Is that not wonderful?"

His eyes narrowed. "You saw Warren, and you are leaving with him?"

"Yes." She stopped bouncing and contained herself, looking him in the eye.

"You saw Warren? Where?" His jaw set.

She pursed her lips, hand waving dismissively. "He heard I was here and came early this morning. I went for a drive with him and just returned."

"And where is he now?" Theo asked.

"He had to go home and pack his necessities." A bit of the enthusiasm dropped out of her tone.

He crossed his arms in front of his chest. He studied her as she moved toward the door. "I *do* have friends, you know."

"Is that a threat?" she hissed, not fully turning back.

He crossed the deck and closed the space between them, his hand going straight for her throat, pinning her against the wood siding of the house. "It is now."

She choked as she attempted to speak, her hands gripping his as she tried to free herself. "Have you lost your mind?"

"Where is she?"

Kay looked at him with pleading eyes. "Please stop, Theodore. You're going to kill me."

"I won't ask again. Where is she?" His grip tightened.

The flesh beneath his hand shifted as the image in front of him changed. The hair came down, cascading over his fingers. The body filled out with a bit more muscle. The facial features became more hardened. While female, the woman he was holding to the wall was no longer Kaori.

She sneered. "Why do you care so much? You barely know her."

"Did you know her at all before you chose to condemn her to whatever fate your boss has for her?" He loosened his fingers but didn't let go.

She coughed beneath his palm, all signs of her amusement gone. "Just let it go, Theodore."

"Let's try this another way." He gripped her hair, finally releasing her neck. "Who are you? Other than Porter's little lackey."

Her knees buckled slightly. Nails dug into his arms as she reached up, gripping his arm to steady herself. "Let's just say, you can just think of me as a ghost."

She transformed into a fox, writhing in his grip. Her teeth sunk into his hand, and he let go, pulling his bleeding palm up to his chest. "You little . . ."

She scrambled off the deck with him running after her, but her tiny frame skittered under places he couldn't. Finally, almost a mile into the woods, after jumping over piles of brush, ducking under branches, and cursing the entire way, Theo stopped.

Sniffing, he worked to pick up the kitsune's scent. He cursed himself for letting his tracking skills go slack with his mundane life. He was just about to give up when he caught her scent and darted in its direction.

CHAPTER 6

Kaori woke, her head aching worse than the strongest hangover she'd ever experienced. She tried to sit up, but the room spun in such a sickening way that she fell back against the pillow and rolled onto her side, hand covering her mouth.

"It should pass shortly. Sorry to bring you here this way." A man's voice came from somewhere in the room.

She attempted to look for him as the wave of nausea subsided. "What's going on? Who are you? Why am I here?"

The man chuckled. "You're not unlike her. So many questions."

Kaori's head was starting to clear. She sat up and propped herself against the wall. "Are you going to answer any of them?"

"It's no wonder he fell for you." The man took a seat in the chair next to the door, legs crossed and arms folded across his chest. He waited a moment before going on. "My name is Porter Patterson. You're here to help your family."

At that, she leaped up. "My family? Are they in trouble? If something has happened, all you needed to do was tell me. I would go to their aid. I didn't need to be convinced to do so." She was looking around for her shoes and any belongings. "What has happened? And I still would like to know who you are."

A look of amusement washed over him as he watched her. "I like you. We're going to get along great, once you learn your place."

She stopped, leaning over to peer under the bed she woke up on to see if her things were under there. With one hand on the mattress, she slowly lifted up halfway, her eyes fixed on the floor beneath her. "Learn what?"

"Come. Join me in the sitting room. Once Emiko returns, we will explain everything." He started for the door.

Standing up fully, Kaori balled her fists.

"What is going on?" She punctuated each word.

He waved casually, signaling for her to follow. "As I said, once Emiko returns, you will find out. Until then, come have a brandy with me. We might as well get on more friendly terms."

"Friendly terms? You drugged and kidnapped me! You're not going to get hatefully pleasant out of me!" she roared.

Kaori hadn't seen him move. She blinked, and suddenly, he was nose to nose with her. Not touching, but she could feel his warm breath on her face as he spoke. "You'd be wise to cooperate. Once you find out why you're here, you will certainly change your tune. But until then, do not make me teach you what I can do to unruly kitsune."

"You know what I am?" She sucked in a breath. "Are you—"

"No," he spat. "I am *not* one of you cruel beasts. But I know all about your lineage."

He spun and stormed out of the room. Kaori watched. Fear had crawled up from the pit of her stomach and was strangling her throat, threatening to cut off her ability to breathe. She couldn't move. She just stared at the doorway he exited through, unsure if she should, in fact, join him or stay in that room. Unable to think clearly, she just stood there, her thoughts spiraling out of control.

Kaori had no concept of how much time had passed when a figure entered the doorway. She looked at Kaori with a deep sadness that was plain on her features, pinching what was clearly a beautiful face into one that was weary and deeply hurt. The woman gathered herself, breathing away the expression in exchange for a colder one, then spoke. "Kaori Ishida?"

Kaori looked at her blankly. "Yes?"

"Follow me, please." Her voice was melodic.

"Are you Emiko?" Kaori started to come out of her daze.

The woman didn't look back. She paused. "Follow me," she said, then continued walking.

"Wait!" Kaori ran to catch up. She grabbed the woman's shoulder, tears in her eyes. "If you're Emiko, please tell me what's going on."

"I am Emiko." She swallowed hard, then lifted Kaori's hand off her shoulder, letting it drop, still unable to look at her. Clearing her throat, her words came out slightly choked. "Follow me."

"Why does everyone seem to want me to just blindly follow them?" Kaori bellowed.

Emiko gritted her teeth. "Suit yourself, but you won't want to deal with him if you don't."

Kaori watched as Emiko walked out of the room, turning down the hallway to the right, the same direction Porter had gone. Her feet felt like cement bricks, keeping her in place. Still not wanting to leave the room, she wrapped her arms around herself and took a few deliberately steady breaths.

Her mind becoming slightly less foggy, she peered out the door. Once she was sure nobody was there, she retreated back into the room, transformed into a fox and started sniffing the walls, looking for a way out.

Going the opposite direction from Porter and Emiko, she made her way to the staircase and down. All the windows were closed, and nobody else seemed to be in or around the house. Still, Kaori made sure to make as little noise as possible.

The front entry was massive. Two solid, ornately carved wood doors loomed over her in her fox form as she studied them. Though she wanted so badly to turn back into her human form, burst through the doors, and run outside and away, something made the hairs on her neck stand up.

Turning away from the doors, afraid of making too much noise, she made her way back to the kitchen, sniffing for hints of the various scents of food that might be there. She slowly creeped in, making sure it was devoid of people. Once sure, she went in, passing counters and appliances on her way to the door off the back of the house.

She looked up at the doorknob, readying herself to grip it the moment she transformed. Just as she was about to, a hand gripped her scruff and lifted her up into the air. "Now, now, Miss Ishida. I do believe that I asked you to join me. Your manners seem to have escaped you."

Kaori let herself go limp in his grip, knowing that anything else would risk him lashing out at her physically. As he turned with her in hand, she caught a glimpse of Emiko standing there with Kaori's dress and shoes in hand. Her eyes were cast down.

An unexplained pang of empathy for Emiko shot through Kaori, but before she could figure out why, Porter yanked her down the hall and into the study, tossing her down onto a chair. "I'll turn around while you get dressed . . . as a human." His words were pointed.

Emiko tossed the items onto the floor next to the chair and turned so her back was to Kaori. "Make it quick, please."

Kaori sat in the chair, looking back and forth between her captors. Her gaze falling past them, she calculated a few options of attempting to escape—all of which ended with it not going her way. She let out a snort, her little nose twitching, before she reluctantly phased back into human form, then quickly reached over, grabbed her clothing, and slid into her dress.

Feeling violated, she wrapped her arms around herself before announcing her transformation. "I'm human again. Well, as human as I can be. Can you *please* explain to me what is going on now?"

Turning and taking their seats casually, Porter and Emiko sat, poised, as if conducting a business deal, not addressing someone they'd just kidnapped. Porter's arrogance came through in his movements, while Emiko's attitude reflected a clear reservation and a sorrow.

Porter straightened a pile of papers on his desk. "So Emiko here has been my companion for a number of years."

"Centuries. Three centuries," she corrected him.

"Yes. Three centuries," he agreed, speaking through his teeth. He relaxed his jaw and continued. "And I've agreed to let her go if she were to find a replacement for herself."

"And you think that replacement is going to be me?" Kaori stood. "Absolutely not!"

"But you haven't heard the pay, Miss Ishida." He sat in his office chair, tapping an envelope opener on the desk, amused.

She stayed standing, her hands on her hips. "With how you brought me here, I cannot imagine that you could propose any amount of pay that would entice me to stay and be some sort of companion for you."

"You'd be surprised," Emiko said, almost under her breath.

"Please, sit." He nodded to Kaori.

He waited and let her take a moment to stay there, defiantly, before finally sitting back down. Emiko's lips were pursed as she watched the other woman, an eyebrow quirked. As Kaori sat, she rolled her eyes, then turned and waited for Porter to continue.

He started to explain. "Just over three hundred years ago, I was a young, budding priest. The Christian god infiltrated everything I did and felt. And one year, I was selected to go on a pilgrimage from my home in France all the way to the Orient to spread the word. It was a wonderful trip, since I'd never been there, and it was my first time being selected to go on such a journey. I'll admit, I got a little overzealous. And despite it being illegal and dangerous to practice Christianity in Japan, I wanted to bring enlightenment to the world. So I went.

"I met a girl," he continued. "She was exotic, enticing, and undeniable. At least she was to me. So one night, I took her to my bedchamber. In exchange for showing me carnal pleasures, I told her all about my god and church. But come morning, that bitch had told both the Japanese government as well as my church elders what had happened between us."

He flashed a scathing look at Emiko before setting his jaw. "I took refuge in a cave a few miles outside of town, knowing that the local government would imprison me for my religion, or possibly worse. Then there was the matter of my elders. I was not sure what my church would do to me. So I hid. And who do you think I saw out there in those woods? The very young woman that had me out in that cave. She went by the name Tamao."

"Tamao?" Kaori gasped. "As in . . ."

"Our cousin," Emiko answered her question.

"*Our*? Wait. What do you mean?" Kaori looked back and forth between the two of them, anxious for an explanation.

Porter waved his hand dismissively. "Yes, Tamao was romping around in the forest—naked. She'd transformed from her fox form and was picking berries and flowers, putting them in a basket. I didn't know what was going on at first. At least, not until Emiko here joined Tamao. She approached as a fox and transformed, giggling and helping her cousin with the berries while they laughed about the man Tamao had turned in. They were bragging about the line of men they would seduce and turn in to authorities, ruining their lives and even sentencing some to their deaths."

Kaori's face contorted with fear and anger. "Emiko? You're my cousin, Emiko? The Emiko my family said had run off like so many others?"

Emiko nodded coldly. "Yes. That's what they say when someone disappears, isn't it? If only you knew the truth behind so many of those disappearances. Most are *not* a simple case of wanderlust. That's for sure."

Porter interjected. "Before we get all mushy with the rest of the family reunion between you two, allow me to finish my story."

Emiko folded her hands in her lap as Kaori sat upright. "All right. Finish."

"Thank you." He smiled and nodded. "So I took my cloak and snuck out, draping it over the frolicking women. Emiko, being the spry one of the two, escaped my grasp. Tamao, on the other hand, did not. She *did* try to change back into her fox form, but that just allowed me to wrap her up even more. And once little Emiko here saw that her dear cousin was without hope of escape, she was sweet enough to come back for her. Standing in front of me with every bit of her flesh for me to see, she demanded I let her go."

"I didn't care if you saw me like that. I was trying to save my cousin," Emiko snarled.

"Watch your tongue," Porter scolded her, his eyes changing from poised and pleasant to angry and threatening. He regained his composure quickly, though, and returned to his story. "I told Emiko that I was going to turn in their family—your family—for not only being scandalous sluts, but also for the fact that I'd seen them turn into humans from their fox shapes. Sure, Emiko questioned me as to how, since I was more or less a wanted man. But I kindly explained that this sort of thing would get me off the hook with my elders in the church, and that mattered far more than anything else. I would simply have to explain that Tamao cast a spell upon me, and I had no control over my actions. But more than that, they would most assuredly go after every one of your kind, starting with your family. And we would start by burning Tamao at the stake for witchcraft."

"You're a monster." Kaori felt ill.

"I am a man of survival," he replied smugly. "Now, mind you, the night Tamao and I spent together, she told me tales of beings with a variety of capabilities. She spoke of changing from animals to humans. She spoke of sensing another's presence, changing a person's moods, and far more. When I learned that her tales were true and that she was speaking of her family, it became obvious to me I needed to keep them both and see what they could do for me. One power, in particular, was of great interest to me. She explained that some had the ability to feed a mortal life force to keep them alive. And do you know what she did?"

"Obviously not escape." Kaori's words were full of venom.

"No, she did not." Porter raised an eyebrow. "Tamao bargained with me. She said she would give me some valuable information in exchange for her freedom." He roared with laughter. "And when I agreed, she explained that her very own cousin, Emiko, had that very ability. Emiko didn't deny this, of course. She agreed to provide me with immortality and aid me in some business pursuits in exchange for her cousin's freedom and the survival of your family."

Kaori choked back her churning stomach. "What?"

"To save your ungrateful lives," Emiko growled.

Porter waved his hand, signaling for her to back off. "Once I had Emiko's promise to come with me in exchange for your family's safety, I kept them both, making sure Emiko understood that her cousin's safety was still at risk unless she showed me a few of her tricks."

"You kept them both? But you had an agreement. How could you go back on that?" Kaori was stunned.

He shrugged. "I had a promise but no evidence. I needed to know for sure. And I needed an insurance, so to speak. Tamao wasn't going to get off the hook that easily, even if Emiko was going to take her place."

Kaori grimaced. "How could you help this monster all these years, Emiko? Certainly you could have done something!"

"How could I? *How could I?*" Emiko rose, her fists balled tight. "I did what I had to do to save us!"

"She did what she knew was best," he added.

Kaori went to speak again, but Emiko cut her off, stepping forward while waving a finger at her. "Don't you *dare* judge me. You and I saw firsthand what people of his church did to nonbelievers. Remember? Remember how we had to watch them drag people out of their homes? There was no way I was going to let them do that—or worse—to our family."

Kaori had to swallow back a swell of emotions. "But why all these years?"

Emiko quickly wiped tears from her eyes before they could fall. "Did you ever second-guess my disappearance? Did you ever try to find me?"

"No?" Kaori replied, confused. "But the elders said that you'd gone off on your own. Was I supposed to track down every family member that decided to go off on their own?"

"That's exactly it!" Emiko raised her voice. "Not a single one of you came after me. Nobody tried to find either Tamao *or* me! And do you know how many others that just 'went their own way' that didn't do it by choice? You haven't even asked where Tamao is, have you? Because she sure didn't come back to the family, did she?"

Kaori's stomach sank. "What happened to Tamao? And what others? What happened to the others?"

Porter approached Kaori and put a hand on her shoulder. "You look a bit overwhelmed. Should we take a break? Maybe get something to eat or drink before you have to take more of all of this in?"

She flung her arm, throwing his hand off of her. "No, I don't want to *take a break*! I want to know what happened to my family! Our elders said people were just going off on their own. I thought people were just living a different life." She looked at Emiko with pleading eyes. "Please. Tell me!"

Emiko looked hardened. The pity and sadness that had shown through her expressions was gone. "Death."

"Death?" Kaori's hand flew to her mouth.

"Wait. Wait. Wait." Porter shook his head. "To be fair, there's a story to each. And each story is linked to Emiko's attempt at escaping or even trying to kill me. It took her well over two hundred years before she figured out that my powers were growing the longer she kept me alive. And by my powers, I mean that she was not only giving me her life force, but in it was the ability to do some things of my own. One of which was being linked to her." He snickered. "Now, of course, I didn't tell her this when I realized it many, many years before she did. And it took her foolish pride quite a long time to clear away and see what was happening. But we've been in a good partnership ever since. Would you say, Emiko?"

He gripped Emiko's shoulder and pinched, causing her knees to buckle slightly. But she held her gaze on Kaori. "Yes. Perfect. Wouldn't wish for a better arrangement."

"That's right." He let her go.

"Tamao? So she's dead?" Kaori's breaths were heavy.

"Tamao?" he repeated. "Oh. No. I forced Emiko to take her to my elders at the church for punishment for attempting to kill me. They are still holding her. Can you imagine? She's been shackled in the basement of their monastery in Italy all these years, being studied and tested by generation after generation of clergymen."

"You let them take her?" Kaori felt her stomach rising once again.

Emiko didn't answer this time. She stood as cold as a stone. Porter, with his ego flaring, explained, "I believe you had a couple of family members disappear together? An uncle and a very young kit, not even able to turn human yet."

The blood drained out of Kaori's cheeks. "You didn't."

"Not for some years." Porter shrugged. "But they were fantastic collateral to get Emiko to take Tamao to the church. But eventually, her antics did cost them their lives . . . and several others. Once I had her ability to sense your kind, it was easy to find others. And with her as bait, they came seeking her."

"And you can be so callous about all of this?" Kaori spat.

He gripped her arm. "I was owed a life that Tamao was so callously willing to take from me."

"You've gotten it many times over with as long as you've lived. And you've taken a number of other lives that didn't owe you a thing." Kaori struggled to escape his grip in vain.

"But if you look at it another way, maybe *this* was the life I was meant to live, and I'll be damned if I let it slip through my fingers. Obviously I wasn't made to be a priest." He chuckled.

"So what do you want with me? Did Emiko step out of line again, and I'm the tool to put her back in?" Kaori looked back and forth between them.

"No. No. This is actually the interesting part." Porter motioned for Emiko to speak.

She hung her head for a moment before looking back up with an anger in her eyes. "I have saved the family long enough. It's someone else's turn."

"You?" Kaori scoffed. "It doesn't sound like you've saved us. It sounds like you've doomed us to millennium of him picking us off one by one!"

Emiko slapped Kaori hard enough to leave a handprint on her cheek. "I have done the best I could. Without what I've done—what I've sacrificed—you would have all met a far worse fate centuries ago. So don't pretend like I'm the villain here!"

Kaori's hand flew up and held her burning cheek, a little stunned by her cousin's action. "What now? Obviously he isn't going to just let you go and let himself wither away. Am I the collateral for making you stay this time?"

"No." She slumped into a chair. "You're my replacement."

"Me?"

Exhaustion pulled her shoulders down. "I remember, when I was a very young kit, you had fallen in love with a human. A young man you'd met on the docks of Kyoto. A sailor, if I remember correctly. And you refused to let him go. It was a huge scandal that he lived for so long with such a young appearance, never seeming to age. Whispers turned to fact when it came out that you could keep other creatures alive."

"Ryu Saito," Kaori said, solemnly.

"Yes. Ryu," Emiko repeated. "It was known then that you had the gift like mine. So it's your turn, *itoko*."

Kaori took a step toward Emiko. "*Itoko*? How dare you even consider yourself family, let alone my cousin! You are a traitor to our family!"

"A traitor?" Emiko screamed. "I have sacrificed over three hundred years of my life to keep as many of you safe as I could! Sure, I've made mistakes that have cost lives, and I have to live with that. Trust me, it haunts me every single day. But I'm done. I want to live. So I brought you here to take my place." She looked over to Porter. "You have her. Please let me go. I have no desire to spend another moment going over this. You have what you want—my replacement. Now please, let me go."

Kaori's eyes went wide. "Wait. What do you mean you brought me here? You mean earlier, when you drugged me, right? Did you have something to do with Warren's disappearance? Where is he? Is he harmed?"

Porter held a hand out to Emiko, signaling for her to stand down as he waited for Kaori's string of questions to stop. Once she was finished, he turned his hand over, as if presenting Emiko. Kaori's eyes slowly shifted back to her cousin and went wide, her face stark white as Emiko shifted and changed into Warren.

Kaori breathed, "No." Tears started streaming down her cheeks. "How could you?"

Emiko turned back into her American appearance, her head turned down. "I couldn't cost another life."

"Cost another life?" Kaori angrily wiped her cheeks. "You came for *my* life, yet you say you couldn't cost another life? That's a bit backward, isn't it?"

Emiko didn't reply. Porter, on the other hand, nodded to the doorway before putting a hand on Kaori's shoulder once again. "Now, dear, do you really think I would let her go off to Japan to retrieve you without a reason for her to return?"

Reaching up, Kaori pushed Porter's hand off of her with disgust on her face. "What did you do with the others in our family you murdered? Why didn't you just get me here like you did them?"

"Taking members of your family was far easier back when we lived much, much closer. When we moved to America, Emiko attempted to betray me once. I'm sure you remember several of your family members going off on their own about a hundred years ago, outside of Kitsuki—a name I have chuckled at, considering the closeness of your kind's name and the district's name. Is that on purpose?" He tilted is head.

Kaori's nostrils flared. "Are you serious right now?"

"Yes," he stated, plainly.

She just looked at him, completely shocked at his audacity.

Finally, he waved off his inquiry. "Fine. A question for another time. It's not like we don't have plenty of that—time. But back to story time. Since I'd seen your family's migration patterns, it didn't take much to predict where they'd be. And considering that Emiko's little stunt spurred our trip back to Japan to remind her of her place, I slit one neck in front of her and sent five other little kitsune to join Tamao, thanks to a young, eager priest who kept my secret of my long life in exchange for taking the credit for finding them. Oh!" He almost leaped at recalling something as he practically bounded out of the room, calling back, "Don't move, ladies. I nearly forgot your surprise."

Kaori cringed at Porter's sing-song tone in his voice. She looked over at Emiko, her words hissing through her teeth. "What *surprise*?"

Emiko paced. "I don't know."

"Do *not* play stupid, *itoko*!" Kaori shouted.

"I *don't know*!" Emiko's fists were balled. "He takes great joy in his tortures."

"Joy? And this is the life you want to condemn me to?"

"You all left me to this life without any hope of rescue. I may have chosen it in the beginning, but I prayed one of you would come for me."

"Emiko, I thought you were fine. I thought you chose to leave us!"

"You should have known I hadn't." Emiko rubbed her forehead.

"How could I have known that?" Kaori started to close the gap between them.

Stopping and putting her hands out, not letting Kaori get any closer, Emiko swallowed back tears. "We were too close for you not to know. All I ever talked about was the future of our family and how much I loved you all. What could have possibly changed my mind so swiftly?"

"The elders believed you all had been thinking about it for some time and finally took action." Kaori clasped her hands in front of her heart. "The elders said we were not to go looking for anyone and risk the family. And I blindly did as they said."

"The elders are cowards. And you were so willing to follow a man, yet you were not willing to come look for your closest cousin? Your best friend?" Emiko pursed her lips.

Kaori closed her eyes. "I believed them."

"And I will never forgive you for it. You should have known." Emiko stormed across the room and stared out the window.

The two women stood, tense, quiet, Emiko holding her anger back, and Kaori completely lost. Their silence broke with Kaori's gasp as she saw Porter re-enter the room with a man by his side. "Kai?"

Emiko whipped around. "Kai!" She ran across the room and stopped short of the two men. "What is this, Porter? I've done what you want. I brought you my replacement."

Kai stood, his hands bound behind his back, ankles shackled, his mouth gagged. He was covered in bruises and a number of cuts, some still bleeding. His hair was long, shaggy, and dirty, matching his clothes that were torn and covered in filth. It was obvious they had once fit him but just hung on him now.

Emiko fell to her knees. "Please, Porter. No!"

"Can you imagine Kai's excitement when he learned Emiko was alive, and he could come to where she was? But his disappointment rivaled that excitement when he figured out that he wasn't going to see her." Arrogance laced Porter's words.

Kai struggled under his gag, trying to speak. Porter kicked the back of his knees, causing Kai to fall painfully to the ground. Emiko dove forward, sobbing. "Stop! Please stop!"

"You see, Kaori? Emiko sacrificed a lot. And while I cannot bear to see her go—nor can I risk her being free, knowing my secrets—I figured I'd bring him here as well. Now I have three of you!" He clapped his hands. "We can be one big, happy family!"

Emiko crawled across to Kai, her hand on his cheek. She looked up at Porter. "What do you mean, can't let me go? We had an arrangement! And how did you find Kai? Or even know about him?" Her words were choppy around her sobs.

Porter knelt down next to the two, blocking Emiko from getting to Kai. "It's amazing what you learn about someone over three hundred years with them, connected to their energy. When we went back to Japan that last time, your heart fluttered when you saw him. Sensing his species, thanks to you, Emiko, I knew that he would come in very handy."

She looked up at him in horror. "You've had him this entire time?"

Porter reached out and stroked her hair. "The church has had their little experiments. I wanted the chance to test a few things out on my own, and I needed you for all your errands. So Kai has been helping me with some scientific research, so to speak."

Emiko sprang up and lunged at Porter. Her hands wrapped around his neck as she pushed him back and into the nearby archway frame. His breath left him as he hit, catching him completely off guard. He scrambled, trying to get a grip on her and push her off of him.

Kaori rushed over to Kai, who was pulling at his restraints. She untied his gag and started working on the knots in the rope around his wrists. Every bit of her wanted to see who was winning the scuffle, but she wasn't sure she was safe either way. She kept her attention on the knot as anxiety rose into her throat the closer she was to untying it.

She felt the tension in the knot finally give. Fumbling with the newly slack rope, she started to pull the loosened knot apart. Then everything went black.

CHAPTER 7

*T*heo chased after the scent for several miles before slowing. He stood, taking in his surroundings, calming, frustrated that he'd lost her. His hands came up to his face, rubbing it as he shook his head.

He pulled his hands back when the cloud of anger cleared. This time, he looked around to determine his exact location before starting off north. The tree branches scraped him as he ran, leaping over large rocks, dodging bushes, and launching off fallen trees. He only stopped when he came to a clearing at the edge of a neatly landscaped plot of land.

He stood, looking over the gardens and house, evaluating the terrain and its inhabitants. Then, hastily, he gathered some twigs, placing them in a circle at the tree line. He left the foliage on the last two small branches, and placed them one crossed over the other in the center of the circle, before going back into the woods and digging for several small rocks, a young pinecone, and other items.

Returning to the circle, he placed them deliberately around it. He pulled out a pen from his pocket. Recalling that Kaori had used it the day before in his office, her energy still resonating within its metal components, he laid it across the center twigs.

Theo knelt and raised his hands, palms down, over the

arrangement and closed his eyes. He took in long, deep breaths again, this time searching for energy signals of other beings on the property with a focus on Kaori's in particular. His fury and fear both attempted to cloud his ability to focus, so he had to work harder than he ever had before in order to achieve something he'd been taught as a kid. Finally, he zeroed in past his emotions and let the incantation within him take control.

Kaori's energy washed over him like a strong wind, pushing him back onto the ground. He struggled to keep his grasp on the others' as he leaned up on his elbows. Moving back onto his knees, he put his hands down on the dirt on either side of the circle. Kaori's energy was strong still, but he filtered around her and could tell that, among several humans moving about inside and outside of the house, Kaori herself was in a room with two others with similar energy footprints. Theo could feel that she was there with one man he could tell was Porter Patterson, and he growled.

Brushing the twigs and stones aside so as not to leave it to be found, Theo scanned the yard. Once positive no one was within sight, he ran for the house, tucking himself in behind a line of hedges that ran along the south wall, then began to check each window. If the curtains were pulled open, he peered inside to make sure the room was empty before testing the window, moving on as he found them locked.

Then he froze.

Theo looked inside the large picture window just before the corner to the front of the house. It took everything he had not to crash through it in that moment. There was Kaori, lying on the floor, appearing unconscious. There was a man on the floor close to her who seemed to be tied up. Porter was standing over the man with a gun pointed to his head. He was shouting at a woman who was lifting Kaori up by the shoulders, dragging her to the couch.

Hastily, Theo bent down and placed his hands on the earth, drawing as much extra energy as he could before standing back up and placing those hands on the side of the house. He listened, trying to assess what was going on inside.

Again, his focus faltered. And again, he tried to regroup to get past it. But seeing Kaori like that had him fighting with his savage side. The urge to burst into the room, kill everyone else in it, and carry her out was so overwhelming that he had to take a break, lean his back against the siding, and put a block up—to wall himself in and isolate his mind from the world around him.

~

Kaori's head pounded when she came to. Her hand went up, feeling the lump on her scalp where she'd been hit. She sorted through the events that had unfolded before she'd been knocked out, not sure if Emiko or Porter had been the one to do it. So when Emiko stood from the chair across the room, Kaori jumped.

Emiko held her hands up. "Relax. I'm locked in here just like you."

Kaori squinted. "So you weren't the one to render me unconscious?" She flinched as she tried to sit up.

"No," Emiko replied.

"What happened, then?" Kaori asked. She looked around, seeing they were still in the study, but the doors were all closed, and there was no sign of Porter or Kai.

"He took him." Emiko folded her arms across her chest and looked off at the fire in the stone fireplace. "He knocked you out, pulled out a pistol from his waistband that I didn't even know he had on him, and threatened to shoot Kai if I didn't back down." Emiko swallowed hard. "I carried you to that couch, and he locked us in here, taking Kai with him."

Kaori held her head with both hands. "So let me get this straight. You tried to save Tamao's life and everyone in the family by taking Tamao's place in his revenge, but he took you both. She's locked in some dungeon, being tortured while you've been forced to do lord knows what for over three hundred years, keeping him alive through our magic, costing several lives when you'd attempt to kill him or escape, instead of coming and telling the elders so they could take care of it?"

Emiko started to speak, but Kaori cut her off. "And *now*, you thought you were sick of it finally and, instead of killing him or—again—coming to our elders, you track me down and trick me into thinking that you're someone else, making me fall in love with that fictional person and follow a lie to America, only to be lured into this trap. And you *didn't* think he would keep us both? Do I have this right?"

"Close enough." Emiko's tone was full of venom.

"What were you *thinking?*" Kaori shouted, then regretted it right away. Her head started pounding harder. The pulsing of the pain brought her up to her feet, and she paced as she rubbed her forehead.

"I *thought* I was doing the right thing," Emiko shot back. "I was young and scared. I had no clue he was this much of a monster. And I never, in my worst nightmares, thought it would go on for this long."

Kaori pinched the bridge of her nose, the thudding pain slowing a little. "I'm sorry I never went looking for you."

Emiko's jaw set. "It doesn't matter anymore."

"Yes, it does." Kaori stopped, her back to the window. "What you said was right. We *were* close. I should have known you better. I just blindly trusted our elders to not lie. And I still don't understand why that would be their reaction if you'd just disappeared. Why didn't *they* go looking for *any* of you who had disappeared?"

Emiko shook her head, disgusted. "I once heard, when I was little, that the elders would always use that as an explanation for any disappearance. My great-grandmother said it was to protect the family. They felt that looking for people would draw attention to our kind and put us in danger."

"So they'd rather just let people go missing than be a true family and find them? To help them?" Kaori felt nausea roll up into her stomach.

Emiko looked right at her. "Yes."

"So you knew that this would happen when you agreed to go with Porter?" Kaori covered her mouth.

"Yes," she replied plainly.

"And you hoped I'd know better and would come regardless?" Kaori asked.

"Not at first." Emiko wrung her hands. "At first, I was settled in my decisions and hoped you would stay away . . . to stay safe. But over the years, I grew resentful toward the family . . . the entire family. Even more so toward you, since I thought you'd see through it one day and come help me like you used to help me when we were young. How you used to get me out of jams when whatever little prank I'd pulled backfired and got me into trouble. But when you never came, I grew to hate you for abandoning me."

"I didn't abandon you, Emiko." Kaori ground her teeth. "You should have come to me. You should have let me help you instead of letting him take you. And even if you couldn't have gotten out of that then, you should have come to me this time instead of luring me here like this!"

"Like I said, I grew to hate you. I didn't trust that you would help me. I just wanted my freedom." Emiko's voice went cold again.

"Damn it, Emiko! You've doomed me to the same fate! You cannot expect me to just accept it!" Kaori shouted.

"No, I don't." Emiko turned away.

Kaori threw her hands up. "And yet, you meet me with such disdain and callousness?"

Emiko turned. "What? Should I have buddied up to you right before I was to leave you to that monster? Should I let all those warm family feelings surface so it could kill me even more when I walked away, knowing I was leaving you to suffer what I have for so long?"

"No. But—"

"But what?" Emiko turned away again. "Nobody wins in this scenario. Being closed off is the best for me, no matter what. I tried to do the right thing, but it cost me everything. It's cost people their lives. So excuse me if I seem a bit disconnected and distant, dear cousin. No matter what I do, it's not going to be right."

"You should have come to me!" Kaori clenched her fists.

Emiko ran her hands through her hair. "Do we need to keep reliving this? I didn't, all right? I didn't go to *anyone*! And through him, I'm a con artist, an impersonator, and a murderer. And yet, with as many gifts as we have, I still can't seem to go back in time to change *any* of it."

Kaori turned and looked out the window. Before she could say anything more to Emiko, she jumped back, almost stumbling over the chair nearby, covering her mouth to stifle a scream. She hit the floor with a thud, sending a shooting pain through her hip. "Theo!"

He motioned for her to stay quiet, looking around to make sure he was still not spotted. Scrambling to her feet, Kaori rushed over and tried to unlock the window, but it wouldn't budge. She looked down at him and shook her head, mouthing, "It won't open."

He attempted to move the frame to no avail. He tapped and waved his hand, signaling for her to stay put.

She looked confused.

He mouthed, "Get back," as he pulled his shirt off and wrapped it around his elbow.

Kaori moved several steps away from the window, giving plenty of distance between herself and the glass, calling over to Emiko as quietly as she could, "Stay back!"

He rammed the glass, shattering it. Scraping the frame free of larger shards, he waved them over. "Hurry! Someone *had* to have heard that. Let's get you out of here."

Kaori ran for him. "Come on, Emiko!"

"You trust her?" he asked as he helped her through the opening.

"I'll explain later." She jumped. "Emiko! Come on!"

"I can't." Emiko backed up against the fireplace mantel.

Kaori reached in. "What do you mean, you can't? This is your chance!"

"Don't you see, Kaori? I can't! He'll kill everyone we love, starting with Kai! I need to stay." She looked away.

"We can come back for him. Maybe even bring help. Please, Emiko!" Kaori pleaded with her cousin.

Theo started pulling Kaori with him. "We need to go."

Her brows pulled in with worry. "I can't just leave her here, Theo. I just can't!"

"If we stay any longer, we might not be able to leave." He scanned the yard again.

Emiko ran to the window. "Go! Now! I've had three hundred years of this. I'm used to it. And if me staying saves you and Kai? Then it's worth it as much as it was when I agreed to go with him back then. Now go!"

"Please!" Kaori put her hand on Emiko's.

Emiko shouted, "She's escaping!" Then turned back and spoke low. "Go! Now!" She yanked her hand back and went for the door, banging on it. "Porter! She's escaping!"

Theo lifted a reluctant Kaori over his shoulder and ran for the woods, the branches scraping over them as he ran as fast as he could, not stopping until he reached a clearing by the river. He dropped her onto a fallen tree and started pacing.

"I told you not to go outside by yourself. And that woman," he pointed in the direction they came from, "is *not* someone you can trust. You could have been killed!"

She started sobbing. "But—"

"But nothing! Don't you get it? This isn't a situation that your family can easily help you out of. This entire area is filled with dangerous people, and your friend back there is in deep with one of the worst." He punched a tree. "I might not have been able to save you!"

"I'm sorry, but—"

"Stop." He held a hand out.

She stood, reaching her hands out. "But, truly, Theo. Let me explain."

He ran back over to her, taking her by the arm. "Later. They're coming. We need to go. Now."

CHAPTER 8

After walking a few miles, Theo lifted Kaori again, carrying her a while longer, across a field and up the side of the mountain ridge. Finally, they came across a clearing which held a small cabin on its edge. The windows were dark, and there were no wheel or hoof marks, which gave the appearance that nobody had visited the tiny log home in quite some time.

Theo set her down on the front porch and unlocked the door. They went inside. He blew dust off the lamp next to the door before striking a match out of the box next to it and lighting the oil wick.

Kaori stepped inside and looked around. "Where are we?"

He took the box of matches and lit a couple more lamps. "I built this cabin for two purposes. For emergencies and for my transformations."

"Transformations?" She tilted her head.

He set the box down and patted out the dust from one of the chairs in the living room. "Yes. Remember, I told you I'm a lycan? And for those times I know a transformation is coming, but I don't trust myself out there, I have a cellar under this cabin, away from town, that I can lock myself away in. It's just a precaution, but it's come in handy a few times."

"You have to do that—lock yourself away? How do you get out?"

She took one of the other seats, coughing as the dust bloomed up around her.

"There's no way my hands and fingers in wolf form could ever work a small lock and key. So I hang the key on the wall, and there's a stick on the floor I have to use to get the key once I'm human again. Then I have to unlock it through the bars." He saw her concerned expression. "It's not an infallible setup, but it's worked thus far."

She blinked. "Sorry. I'm just shocked you have to do that. Our fox forms are similar in mentality to us in human form. I can't imagine having to lock myself away to keep myself safe."

"It's not to keep *me* safe," he explained. "It's to keep everybody else safe. I'm not like other wolf shifters, who tend to have more control over themselves in their animal forms. At times, lycan have control like a shifter, but other times, we lose our humanity completely and become . . . predatory."

Her eyes roamed over him. "I see."

"Does that make you afraid of me now?"

"Should I be? Afraid of you, that is," she replied.

"I hope not."

"There are other wolf shifters here, but not like you?"

"There's the Kasun Wolf Pack, and others. Sheriff Kasun's wife is the pack leader. I'm not deeply involved with the pack itself, but I respect their position in town and her authority over our kind. However, my druid blood doesn't allow the tattoo to control my shifting the way it can theirs. Thus, this place." Hoping to put the conversation behind them, Theo grabbed a wooden box from under the chair he was sitting in and went for the door. "I will have to retrieve a change of clothes for you later. But until I can safely, there are supplies in the bathroom you can use to wash up if you would like. I need to secure the property."

"I can help." She touched his arm. "I know it may look like I was helpless back there, but that's just because I didn't expect everything I learned. But I've got my wits about me more now. I'm not helpless."

"I know you're not." He pushed a lock of hair out from in front of her face. "Go. Refresh and relax. I won't be long."

She watched as he exited, pulling on a fresh shirt on his way, and looked around, feeling far more lost than she wanted him to see. In the kitchen, she took a glass out and filled it with water, refilling it two more times before finally feeling like she wasn't parched. She set the glass in the sink and attempted to spot Theo outside as she passed windows on her way to the bathroom, but there was no sign of him. And not seeing him left a pit in her stomach she didn't like.

Kaori shut and locked the door to the bathroom, pulling out the soap and a small towel. She washed quickly, stopping only when she saw the bruise on her cheek from Emiko's slap. A dam broke inside her, and the flood of emotions came rushing over her. She crumpled to the floor, curling around herself. Hot tears ran down her cheeks, soaking the front of her dress.

The door crashed open, wood splintering. Theo came rushing in, dropping to the floor next to her, gripping her by the shoulders. "Kaori! What happened? Are you all right?"

She was shaking, the tears refusing to cease. "I . . . I . . . It was all a lie."

"A lie?" He grabbed the towel and wiped her face. "What was a lie?"

Her sobs broke apart her words as she tried to speak. "All my family members we thought had just gone to find a life away from the rest, many of them were killed. Emiko . . . Emiko wasn't dead. And Warren . . . not real."

Theo lifted Kaori to her feet, wrapping an arm around her. "Come. Let's get you to a more comfortable spot."

He helped her to the couch, taking a seat next to her. Finally, her tears began to slow, as did the hiccupping as she tried to speak. "Emiko is my cousin."

"Your cousin?" He looked shocked.

"Yes." Her breaths were stuttered. "Tamao, another one of our cousins, set Porter up over three hundred years ago. He deserved what she was going to do to him, but he caught on, and he took her and Emiko in exchange for not destroying our entire lineage."

"And Warren?" he asked.

Kaori explained everything, from why Tamao set Porter up to Emiko impersonating Warren to bring her to Havenwood Falls to take her place with Porter. She included Porter informing them that neither would be able to leave and how he had Kai, which was why Emiko refused to go.

Theo stormed back and forth in the small cabin. "So he and his church are keeping some of your family to experiment on them?"

"Yes. He has Kai there now, threatening him if she doesn't stay . . . if *we* don't stay. And now I don't know what he's doing to them because of me escaping." Tears started falling down her cheeks again.

"Since we don't know what all powers he picked up feeding off her life force, we have to be extra careful. But we have to do something, considering that I don't think you'll just let me get you out of town and safe." He rubbed his temples.

"No, I can't just leave her," she insisted.

He gripped her shoulders gently. "But, Kaori, she pulled you into this mess. Because of her, your heart is broken, displaced, and in serious danger."

She put her hand to his cheek. "She's my cousin. And no matter what horrors came out of all of this, she was just trying to do the right thing."

"Dragging you here by pretending to be a man you would fall in love with just so she can force you to take her place is the right thing?" He let his hands drop.

"No." She lowered her hand as well, entwining her fingers together in her lap. "But if I spent over three hundred years in the *jigoku* . . . sorry . . . hell that she has, I might be ready for someone else to carry the burden, as well." She could see him start to speak, to defend his point, but she held a finger up and stopped him. "I do not agree with her choices, but Emiko has always been a more mischievous kitsune. Seeing her now . . . The life has been drained out of her soul. She is a shell of who she once was. I just want to see her be *her* once again. Abandoning her will not help that. It'll only force her to go further down this path."

He took her hands in his. "You have the kindest soul I've ever met, Kaori."

She turned her hands over, wrapping her fingers around his palms. Her eyes met his, and they stayed like that, looking at each other for a moment. The energy exchange between them was almost palpable. Her eyes fluttered as she leaned in toward him.

Theo watched her, his own body reflexively moving in toward hers. Her breath warmed his lips when then were only inches apart. His fingers touched her hair, running through it and down her neck before coming around and resting on her shoulder.

She shivered in anticipation, letting her eyes close fully. She was so swept away, it took her a moment to realize he wasn't touching her anymore. She looked, and he was across the room, pouring himself a glass of water.

"I didn't mean to overstep," she whispered.

He gulped the water down. "No. It is I who should be apologizing. I shouldn't be taking advantage of your state. I know full well you're fragile right now."

"Fragile?" She furrowed her eyebrows. "I'm not fragile."

The glass clinked as he sat it in the metal basin. His hands planted on the side of the counter, he took in a breath. "You learned so much today that has got to have you shaken. I can't imagine how you're not falling apart right now. And it's wrong of me to burden you any further."

She crossed the room and stood behind him. "But you're not a burden. You've helped me in so many ways. You've been . . ."

"In the wrong." He gripped the edge of the counter harder.

Kaori reached out and touched his shoulder. "Theo—"

He growled. "Warren."

"Warren?" She reeled back. "Warren was a lie. He wasn't real. I told you that."

"But you must be heartbroken. You were so in love and excited to see him." His expression was pinched.

"I am over five hundred years old, Theo. He was a lie, and I won't spend my life dwelling on that. It's hard enough for me to let someone in as it is. I will process my anger for what Emiko has done and, more so, what Porter has done. But I don't shed tears for someone who didn't even exist, beyond that first moment of finding out. Period. I followed Warren because I felt fate calling me. I thought he was it. But sometimes fate isn't what it seems." She touched his shoulder again, letting her fingers brush down his arm before turning and walking away.

Theo let out a low, deep, guttural growl. The sound of wood creaking came from where his hands were pressing into the wood of the counter. He let go, whipped around, and caught up with Kaori in only a few paces. He spun her around and pulled her in. Placing his hands on her cheeks, Theo pressed his lips against hers.

Kaori's arms went up, wrapping around his shoulders, her fingers entwining in his hair. His hands slid down her sides, and gripping her thighs, he lifted her up. Colliding with the wall, he pressed against her. Her fingers slipping up under his shirt, she pushed it up and over his head. Moans escaped their lips, accompanied by growling from Theo as their passion grew.

With one arm holding her up, Theo moved them over to the bed, tossing the dusty comforter off onto the floor. He laid her down softly, pushing the hair out from in front of her face. His muscular frame looming over her, he let his eyes roam over her figure as she lay beneath him. Her hands went up, fingertips tracing lines down his chest.

"Kaori." His breaths were heavy.

"Yes?" She tucked her fingers into his waistband.

He smirked.

Without saying anything more, his hands gripped the collar of her dress and pulled, splitting the fabric down the front. Her exposed body lying there, he took in her every curve. "You are absolutely beautiful."

She giggled. "Thanks. I made her myself."

He chuckled, remembering her abilities. "Well, you did good."

Her giggle turned into a full laugh. "Shut up and kiss me."

The sun was coming in through the break in the curtains, warming Kaori's face when she woke. A smile played on her lips as flashes from the night before ran through her head. She yawned, stretching her arms up over her head as she rolled over. A rush of panic ran through her when she saw the other side of the bed empty.

She sat up, pulling the sheet up around her to cover herself. Her dress lay torn on the floor next to the bed. Dropping her feet onto the floor, she stood and made her way to a nearby wardrobe. As quietly as she could, she opened the door and looked through the few articles of clothing inside.

"Crap." She sighed as she pulled out a long-sleeved flannel shirt. "I guess this will have to do."

Kaori tucked the sheet up under her arms to hold on to it as she opened the shirt to put it on. But a gust of wind came in as the door opened, blowing the shirt into her face. Unable to see, Kaori instinctively shifted into her fox form and ran for the open doorway.

"Wait!" a female called out.

Kaori scurried between her feet as fast as she could.

The woman turned, shouting to the running fox that was bolting down the front steps. "I'm Theodore's sister!"

Kaori stopped, turned, and looked at her, sniffing the air and assessing if she'd come alone.

The red-haired woman stepped out onto the porch. "I visit my brother as often as I can, never announced. When I saw a woman's things in the spare room and him not there, I simply came out here to see if he'd locked himself in. Can you imagine my surprise to find him in bed with a woman?"

Her nose working the air still, Kaori stood and watched her as she spoke, slowly approaching the front step.

Lifting the shirt off the floor, the sister held it out. "How about I set this inside, and you can go in to get dressed in private. Let me know once you're human and clothed, and we can start over?" She stepped inside, tossing the flannel onto the arm of the nearby chair before returning to the porch, giving Kaori a wide berth to make it through.

Kaori went in, keeping her eyes on the woman the entire way. Once she was in, the door closed. Kaori paused, still unsure about the entire situation. *What did I do? Did I just walk back inside into a trap? Did I let this strange woman just shut me in here?*

"I understand if you need a moment. Just scratch on the door if you'd rather I open it back up and let you run out into those woods alone. I'd rather you didn't, though. Theo would be furious with me." She walked past the door, casting a small shadow over the light shining through as she did.

Letting out a huff, Kaori shifted back into her human form, tossing the shirt over her head and pulling it down as fast as she could. She took inventory of the items in the small cabin she could use for a weapon, if needed, as well as peeked out the windows to get a feel for the grounds. Once feeling as prepared as she was going to be, she opened the door.

"Hi! I'm Heather, Theo's little sister. You're Kay?" Heather bounded into the doorway with a huge grin on her face.

Kaori jumped back a pace. Eyeing the exuberant woman, she took her hand. "Kay. Yes. Nice to . . . meet you?"

Heather pulled her in for a hug. "Sorry. It's just been ages since my brother has let anyone in. He hadn't even written that he'd met someone. But I suppose there wasn't time, was there? No worries. At least I came for a visit and got to meet you."

"Heather, let her breathe. I already explained she's been through a lot. I wanted you to wait until I came back before you met her." Theo stood in the doorway.

"I know," she playfully whined, "but you were taking *forever*."

Theo kicked his boots on the door jamb, knocking mud off his soles. "I hope she didn't scare you too much." He looked at her, confused. "Umm . . . Kay?"

"Yes?" She blinked.

"Kaori Ishida?" he asked.

"Are you okay?" Kaori stepped back. She froze as she caught a glimpse of herself in the mirror. "Oh no! I . . . I'm so sorry!" She whipped around and put her back to the brother and sister, shifting from the olive skin, jet-black hair, and dark eyes of her Japanese appearance back into the brunette form she'd taken on to be allowed into America.

"Ah!" Heather exclaimed. "I was curious how you hadn't been put back on a boat and sent home."

"I heard about the Immigration Act before I came here. I shifted on my way. I guess being startled brought back old habits."

"Well, either way, you look adorable in my shirt." He put an arm around her and kissed her.

Kaori's cheeks turned red. "I'm sorry. I didn't have anything else to wear.

"Don't be sorry." He kissed her forehead, leaning in. "I may ask you to dress like this when we're alone."

She slapped his chest. "Theo!"

He chuckled. "Heather, Kay. Kay, Heather." He handed Kaori a suitcase. "I went back to the house to check on things and to get you a change of clothes. I'll go back later, once we have a plan, but I feared Heather would get impatient and scare you, so I didn't stay long."

Kaori took the bag. "Thank you. And don't worry about it." She looked at Heather. "I'm just a bit jumpy. I hope I wasn't rude."

Heather giggled. "Not at all. I completely understand." She turned to her brother. "Theo here explained a bit about the situation." She looked back at Kaori. "Looks like I came just in time to help."

"To help?" It was Kaori's turn to look confused.

"Yeah!" Heather made her way over to one of the chairs and plopped down on it. "But I guess I need more details than my brother meeting you by chance to clear up a favor for some scoundrel, and the moment he saw you, he knew he—"

He cut her off. "I knew something was amiss if Porter Patterson was involved."

"Yes." She smirked. "And that you have a cousin here that you thought was dead, and now you may not be safe. I'm curious how it is all connected."

"I'm still trying to figure that all out myself," Kaori replied. "Theo, I'll make something to eat if you want to tell her. You're probably less discombobulated than I am."

He kissed her again. "Sounds good. You may need this, then." He went out to the porch and brought in a sack. "I also brought some provisions. Again, we will get more later."

She took the canvas bag, gave Heather a nod, and crossed the small room into the kitchen portion.

Heather mock-whispered to Theo, "I like her."

He chuckled. "I do, too."

Kaori spent the next hour cleaning up the kitchen and making a light lunch and beverages while Theo filled Heather in on the details of the situation. Heather, being lively and still wound up from her travels, was animated in her responses.

Once Theo finished, she went to where Kaori was standing and gave her a huge hug. "You poor dear! I can't even imagine how you must feel."

Kaori gently pried herself out of the woman's arms. "That's what your brother said, as well."

Heather grabbed the plates of food and headed back to the living room area. "Well, he might know a bit better than I."

"What do you mean?" Kaori tilted her head at the two of them. She brought in a pitcher of lemonade and a stack of cups.

Heather looked to her brother, handing him a plate. "You want to share your story?"

"Not really," he grumbled, taking the dish of food.

Heather shrugged. "My brother was once taken by another who was not who they said they were. And the tangled mess cost him dearly."

Kaori handed out the cups and took her plate, sitting on the sofa next to Theo. "Is that why you were so angry yesterday?"

"I was angry because you were in danger," he explained. "But yes. The fact that I have been hurt by someone posing to be another just to get something from me, the fact that Porter is involved, *and* the fact that you were hurt—I did everything I could to keep my temper in check."

"I'm so sorry to put you in this position." Kaori curled up against his side. "What happened to you, and how did you get out of it all?"

"My brother has never let anyone in easily, not even family," Heather jumped in. "That is, other than me. We've always been thick as thieves. That's why I was surprised when I learned he'd been spending time with someone."

"She was a human in a village we had moved to." Theo put a hand on Kaori's knee. "You age significantly slower than us, but as lycan, we age slower than humans. So, as you have had to do, we've had to move around to not be detected. Heather and I moved there first to scout it out. When I started seeing Karen, the rest of our family was concerned about my association with a human, because I wasn't willing to turn her first. So they stayed back."

He continued, "Karen had no powers or anything, but I was sure she reciprocated my emotions. She had recently moved to the small town shortly after we settled in. And as things progressed, I knew I'd have to reveal my other sides to her . . . my were side in particular."

Heather balled her fists. "That stupid b—"

Theo held a hand up, stopping his sister. "In the end, Karen was part of a group of hunters. They had been tracking us for a while. Their plan was to get actual proof, and they knew that if they got close to one of us emotionally, we would reveal who we are. And the moment I did, she tried to kill me."

"She tried to kill you? Right then?" Kaori gasped.

He squeezed her knee reassuringly. "Yes. With it being the full moon, she also had some of her friends nearby. They rushed our home, bringing guns and torches. Heather was shot in the side."

"Thankfully, Theo got me out of there." Heather's hand went to her side, the recollection of the event plain on her face.

"They burned our home, wagon . . . everything. They took our horses and food. I've always had a separate cabin for transitioning away from my home ever since. That night, all I could do was watch from the woods and keep an eye on Heather until she turned back. I took her to a doctor the next morning, then set out to find them." Theo removed his hand, sitting upright as if slightly uncomfortable. "They couldn't bother us after that, but Heather almost died, we lost everything, and our family banished us."

"Banished you?" Kaori's eyebrows pulled in. "They didn't help?"

"They gave us clothes, food, and a few supplies," Heather replied. "Oh, and a couple horses. But that's it. We've not heard from them since and were instructed not to reach out to anyone."

"We've abided by their wishes ever since." He wrapped his arm around Kaori's shoulders, looking over at his sister with an empathetic expression. "When you explained that you'd learned that your family didn't go after those they claimed left for a life on their own, it hit home. I understood the level of betrayal it must have felt for you, because I felt betrayed by our family. We were young. It was a mistake."

"They should have protected us and taken us back in. But no. They left us out in the cold. I don't know any other packs that are so cruel to their members." Heather downed her lemonade and went to the kitchen.

"There may be some, but as a rule, no. Packs stick together through just about everything." Theo turned slightly to face Kaori. "Heather and I have been close ever since. No matter how much she tries to move away and be on her own."

Kaori nodded. "That's exactly it. I'd always thought of our family as nurturing and protective. I don't know other kitsune families, though. Emiko was the brave one. She would sneak out and go play with other foxes when we were just kits. Leaving to come to America to see Warren was the most daring thing I've probably done. And I only did it after my *okaasan* told me to follow fate."

"*Okaasan?*" asked Theo.

Kaori blushed. "Yes. Sorry. My mother."

"Your mother encouraged you? That's so sweet!" Heather returned with a full glass of lemonade. "Getting back to the situation you two have gotten yourselves into, what do we do now? Relocate you both and hope they don't come after you again?"

"No," Kaori snipped. "Sorry. It's just, I can't say I wouldn't have turned into the person Emiko is now, if I were in her situation. We need to help her and Kai. Meanwhile, I'll send word to my family about the others."

"I agree. I don't care what our family did to us. If I knew one of them was in danger, I'd want to help." Theo kissed the top of Kaori's head.

Heather let out a sigh. "Fair enough. But how? If this Porter guy is as dangerous as you say he is, and if Emiko went back to working for him to keep Kai alive, then we'd better have a pretty damned good plan before we do anything."

"Again, I agree," Theo exclaimed. "For now, I need to run the perimeter. Once I'm sure all is set here, if you stay with Kaori,

Heather, I'll go back to the main house. I need to gather more of Kaori's things and some supplies, and I'll come back with the car."

"If Kaori feels safe enough to stay with me." Heather gave Kaori a smile.

She smiled back. "Yeah. I may not have known my cousin's energy, but I'm pretty sure Theo knows and trusts it's you."

Theo laughed. "Yeah. That's my sister for sure."

"But first"—Kaori set her hand on his knee—"food. You can't get all this done on an empty stomach."

"Oh, I *do* like her." Heather roared with laughter. "Finally, I don't have to keep you in line."

Theo threw a chunk of bread at his sister. "Like you've *ever* been the mature one!"

She threw it back. "You're not exactly the pinnacle of adult behavior, mister!"

Both siblings lifted their plates, threatening to throw them, when Kaori stood. "Stop!"

Both looked up at her. "What?"

"I worked hard on those lunches. Do *not* make me mother the both of you. Now eat." She wagged her finger.

"Yup." Heather lowered her plate back onto her lap. "I like her."

Theo took a bite of his sandwich. "Me too."

That night, none of them had come up with a viable plan. Theo, despite his loner status and tendency to handle his own situations, mentioned the Court. He'd been careful to not get entangled with anything that would put him in front of them or even in a situation that went in front of them. However, at a loss for what to do or how to get Emiko and Kai out of there, he suggested they ask for help. The women quickly shot down the suggestion, not wanting to involve others.

Heather leaned away from her brother. "No. You know how we don't like authorities."

"You don't know who is in his pocket, Theo," Kaori added.

"I've not dealt with them much, but I can't imagine that would be the case here," Theo explained.

But Kaori was adamant. "No. Let's do this on our own. I can't tell my family that I got them killed. I just can't. And bringing in people we don't know is risking that."

Reluctantly, Theo conceded. "For now. I'll admit, I'm not one for running to anyone to handle my situations. I was not raised to have others clean up my messes. But I know the Court here. Not informing them of something like this happening in their town could be viewed as a crime. It's a huge risk. So, like I said, for now. But if this can't be easily handled, we tell them. If for no other reason, we will have backup."

"For now," both women agreed.

Heather's journey there had caught up with her. Kaori was exhausted from several days of events. And Theo, still on edge, was hesitant to take action, knowing his anger was still ruling a good portion of his emotions on the matter. So they all stepped away from the topic.

Once Theo returned from the main house, Kaori changed into her own clothes. They sat down to a dinner that Theo and Heather made, forcing a reluctant Kaori to sit, rest, and read for a bit. Theo stoked the fire as the night's chill settled over the woods. The trio sat, reading, curled up with hot cocoa.

There was a looming sense over the three of them that things were going to get worse before they got better. Despite the relaxing atmosphere and sounds of the crackling fire, occasionally one of them would look up and around at the others before checking the doors and windows. The feeling of being on high alert wound through every fiber of the evening.

Finally, feeling Theo's head droop for the third time, Kaori nudged him gently. "Shall we go to sleep?"

"Huh?" he snorted, only half awake. "Sleep? You should get some sleep. Yes."

Heather quietly giggled from her chair.

"Will you come to bed with me?" Kaori patted his leg.

He adjusted, sitting up a bit higher.

She smiled. "I'd sleep better if you would."

He hesitated another moment. "You do need your sleep."

The couple moved from the sofa to the bed as Heather made her own makeshift bed where they'd been sitting. Theo got up one last time and checked the door and windows, then returned to the bed, curling Kaori up against his chest. She nuzzled in and sighed.

CHAPTER 9

$\mathcal{T}$heo's hold on Kaori went slack as he fell asleep. She opened her eyes and checked on Heather, who was fast asleep and snoring softly on the sofa. Something about them both sleeping put Kaori more at ease. She leaned back into Theo's shoulder and drifted off.

"Kaori? Are you here, Kaori?"

"*Okaasan?*" Kaori's eyes began to focus.

She was back in one of the small Japanese villages. A fog was settled over the small town at the base of a mountain. Nobody was around that she could see.

Kaori's mother stepped out from behind one of the nearby trees. "Kaori!" She rushed over and embraced her daughter. "You've had me so worried!"

She hugged her mother tightly, tears welling up in her eyes. "*Okaasan*, I have so much to tell you."

She pulled Kaori back to look at her. "I expected tears but happy tears. These do not look like happy tears, *watashi no kodomo*. Tell me, what has you so troubled?"

"Emiko." Kaori broke down, sobbing in her mother's arms. The leaves of the cherry blossom trees around them rustled in the wind, sending petals across the landscape.

Her mother gasped. "Emiko? I have not heard of your cousin in so very long. If you've found her, should that not be a happy thing?"

"No, *Okaasan*. She is in danger. She told me of how Tamao, many years ago, put our family in a terrible situation. Emiko sacrificed herself, becoming this man's prisoner so he didn't send people to kill us all."

"Is she alive?" she asked.

"Yes. But there's more. There's so much more." Kaori's words broke as she spoke them. "Many have died to keep her with him, and some are prisoner, being experimented on. He's sent some to his church. It is possible Tamao may still be there and alive. Oh, *Okaasan*, I don't know what to do. She won't leave, because he has Kai."

"Kai?" Her mother took her by the hands. "As in Kai Saito? From the Saito kitsune family?"

"Yes, *Okaasan*," Kaori confirmed. "And because he's being held by this Porter Patterson, Emiko would not leave when Theodore rescued me."

"Theodore? Rescue? Murders?" She pulled her hands back and held her head. "My mind is spinning." Quickly, she dropped her hands again, gripping Kaori's upper arms. "Kaori, I feel the waking world pulling at me. You *must* get us all of this in a letter. Every detail that you have learned. It is not possible for us to get there to help save Emiko and Kai. You will have to do what you can. But I will push our elders to go retrieve those being kept at the church." The older woman looked around her as if seeing something. "Please be safe. I love you."

Kaori hugged her mother once again as her image was fading out. "I love you, too, *Okaasan*."

Everything was blurry as Kaori struggled to see, her mind forcing her awake in a panic. She longed to see her mother longer, to get another hug, to get some sort of reassurance that everything was going to be all right. Having that moment with her mother and watching her image dissipate left Kaori with an ache in her chest.

Lifting the comforter off of her, she started to slip out of the bed. She paused, feeling Theo's arm sliding off her side. The cool air seeped in, sending a chill over her skin.

She pulled her feet back under the covers and rolled over, facing him. His hair, slightly curly and disheveled, fanned over his forehead. His breathing was shallow, his breath warm on her as she lay there studying his features.

Kaori pulled his arm back around her, feeling the ache of missing her mother lessen. He stirred, pulling her against him closer. His lips, warm on her forehead, kissed her softly. *"Cadal math mo ghr`adh. Bidh mi gad dh`ion."*

Kaori pressed her lips to his and curled up against his chest. He wrapped both arms around her.

When Theo and Heather woke the next morning, it was to the smell of ham and eggs frying on the stove. Kaori was busily working in the kitchen, making breakfast. Sleep did not come the rest of the night. She lay in Theo's arms thinking over possibilities for getting Emiko and Kai free. Frustrated and not any further toward a plan than the evening before, she chose to get up and put some energy into something else. The scents of her cooking wafted through the small cabin, rousing the others.

"Good morning!" Heather chimed in her singsong voice.

"Good morning, Heather." Kaori handed her a plate of ham, eggs, and potatoes. "Did you sleep well?"

"Yum!" She took the plate. "I did. Thank you."

Theo made his way across the room, snaking his arms around Kaori's waist. "Good morning, doll."

A smile formed on Kaori's lips that she couldn't fight. "Good morning, Theo."

He kissed her neck. "Not going to ask if I slept well?"

Kaori giggled. "Oh. I *know* you slept well. You spoke in your sleep . . . in your native tongue."

His cheeks turned red. "I apologize. I hope I didn't keep you up."

"No." She turned, holding a plate of food out for him. "Whatever you said, which," she put a hand on his chest, "do *not* ask me to repeat. I don't think I could if I tried, but it sounded sweet, and you said it while being very tender. It was perfect timing, since I couldn't sleep."

Theo stepped around Kaori and dished up a plate for her, motioning for her to have a seat. Joining her on the sofa, he took a bite. "Don't worry. We will think of something."

"I spoke with my mother in a dream last night." Kaori's eyes were cast down, the forlorn look returning to them.

"You spoke with your mother in a dream?" Heather sat forward in her chair. "How?"

Kaori blinked. "I don't know, actually. I was taught that I could at a very young age, before I could even turn human."

"Can all kitsune do it with every other kitsune?" Heather asked.

"I've only ever been able to with my mother." Her eyebrows pulled in. "But I've never tried, and I—" She stopped, her shoulders slumping. "I'm learning that I've never asked many questions. I've simply lived as I was taught and told, never truly being curious. I think seeing loved ones leave our family in search of something more, or so I thought, made me not want to be a curious creature. I was happy in my safe little bubble."

"The world is a harsh and sometimes an evil place," Theo said, setting his plate down and turning toward her. "You've been spared some of that torture by having a supportive and loving family. Would it have been right to wage wars and subject everyone to those evils? Or turn your heads and just live, turning a blind eye to it all? Nobody can say what's right and what's wrong. Don't beat yourself up over the past." He ran a hand through her hair. "We just have to focus on what matters."

She placed her hand on his. "You're right. And in our case, fight for a future. I guess that's my struggle—this whole mess is because of things in the past."

"Kaori." He spoke softly.

She looked down. "I know. So what are we going to do? We need to get Emiko and Kai out of there, but are we going to do something

82

about Porter, or are we going to run and hope he doesn't come after us?"

"Tell me about this life force exchange. If Emiko breaks her bond with him, and you're not there to replace her, does he go back to aging normally? Does he have reserves that'll keep him aging slower for a while?"

"His aging will catch up with him faster than a normal human," Kaori explained. "If he would have lived a mere extra ten or even fifty years, it would just shave time off of him. But in his case, three hundred years would probably catch up with him in only a couple years or maybe months. The longer you're kept alive, the faster it comes back on you."

"Can we just lock him in a room and sever their connection so we can watch him age? Give him a small taste of what he inflicts on others?" Heather was leaned back, picking at her nails.

"No," Theo replied with a brotherly, scolding tone. "Knowing this is happening should be enough. We're *not* stooping to his level."

"Fine," Heather dragged out the word. "Don't have to kill him while saving them."

Theo let out a sigh and leaned over Kaori. "My sister has read too many adventure books. I'm pretty sure she would be a pirate if she could."

"The Dreaded Pirate Scott, being from Scotland and all." She laughed. "My reputation would proceed me. But when I arrived to pillage, they'd be shocked I am a woman." She pulled her shoulders back as if proud of her fantasy.

Theo lifted a shoulder. "See?"

Kaori joined in the laughter. "Actually, it's probably needed right now. If we get too serious, we'll probably just mess it all up. Maybe that's our problem. Maybe we're thinking too much, too seriously. Maybe that's why we're coming up with nothing."

"Maybe." Theo picked his plate back up and started eating. "All right, looking at it like that, we simply need to go in and retrieve Emiko and Kai. Then we decide what to do with Porter."

"Okay, but how do we get in for them?" Kaori's shoulders slumped. "That's my biggest roadblock."

"Take a nap!" Heather blurted out.

"A nap?" Kaori was confused.

"Yes! Both of you," she said. "You two take a nap and see if you can communicate. If so, then turn yourself over to Porter tomorrow."

"Absolutely not!" Theo growled.

"Turn myself over?" Kaori blinked.

"Yes. And once you're back inside his house, you can get a good look of who is there and the layout of the house and grounds. See where he's keeping Emiko and Kai. Find out how many people are standing guard. Then, when you sleep, tell all this to Theo in a dream, and we can come after all of you."

"Like I said, absolutely not." Theo had thrown his arm around Kaori protectively. "It's far too dangerous. Why don't you just reach out to Emiko, Kaori?"

"I don't know if I can. I mean, I'm not sure I can even connect with you. I want to save her. She's family, but I still hold my reservations, and that could affect my connection with her. Plus, what if she talks? Can we trust her? Kai doesn't deserve this fate, no matter what she does." Kaori's eyes were full of worry.

"I agree. It's too risky. You and Theo doing this is the best way we have to find out all we need to know in order to wage an attack." Heather looked to Kaori.

Kaori clasped her hands in her lap and looked down.

"That's too risky? But you don't think sending Kaori in by herself is too risky?" Theo almost roared.

Heather glared back at him. "We can trust her. Can you honestly say we can trust Emiko? Kaori, please," Heather pleaded. "He doesn't want to kill you. He wants to keep you."

Theo's anger was boiling over. "Drop it, Heather."

"I'll do it," Kaori finally responded.

"No!" Theo got up and started pacing.

She joined him, placing her hands on his arms. "She's right. It's the best way to get a look at what we're facing."

"But—"

"I can do this." Kaori looked into his eyes.

He returned her gaze, begging her without words to change her mind. They both stood, locked in a silent argument. Seeing she wasn't backing down, Theo winced. "I don't like it."

"She's not some fragile little girl, brother. She's over five hundred years old. I'm pretty sure she's strong enough to handle this. We are the ones who have to be capable of holding up our end and getting them out of there." Heather took her last bite of ham.

Still looking at Kaori, Theo sighed. "I would never forgive myself if something happened to you."

She rested her forehead against his chest. "Then be sure to find me when you sleep so you can come get me out of there."

Theo hesitated, longing to think of some other way to handle things. He stood, mind frozen, stroking Kaori's hair. Coming up with nothing, he growled, a sound deep from within his chest. "Fine. But I don't have a good feeling about this."

Heather patted his shoulder. "We're not asking that you like it." She took her plate out to the kitchen area and washed it. "You two sleep. Let's see if this crazy plan will even work."

Kaori and Theo went to the bed as Heather finished cleaning up the meal, stoked the fire, then sat on the couch. She picked up a book and started to read aloud. The warm fire, calm atmosphere, and overall exhaustion blanketed the couple as they curled up together. It wasn't long before they both drifted off to sleep.

Kaori found herself in an open field. A gentle breeze blew through the delicate blossoms that would, one day soon, become cherries. Fluffy clouds floated by lazily as birds swooped through the sky, playing out aerial shows.

A fallen tree that appeared to have been down for a long time was covered in moss, tall grasses growing up in patches along its bark. Kaori made her way over to it, sitting down and scanning the area. Her shoulders slumped.

"Theo?" She looked around more.

Not seeing him, she felt defeated. She was at a loss for how else to tackle their situation. Determined not to give up, she took the moment to sit in the serene setting and think over a few more possible plans.

"Kaori?"

She felt a hand on her shoulder and jumped.

"Woah! I didn't mean to scare you."

Theo had his hands up as she spun around and saw him. Not hesitating, she thrust herself into his arms and against his chest. "Oh thank goodness! I didn't think it worked!"

He chuckled. "I didn't think I was going to be able to get to sleep. Forcing sleep was a lot more difficult than I expected."

She looked up, smiling. "Hi."

"Hi." He grinned back. "I have to admit, this is"—he rubbed her shoulders while looking up at the trees—"different. I take it this is what your home country looks like?"

Kaori's eyes shone bright. Her arms were wrapped around his waist and her head on his chest as she looked up at him. "Yes. I hope that's all right. I think I'm just used to the setting for my dreams when I meet my mother."

He kissed the top of her head. "It's more than all right. I get to see where you're from. It's perfect."

A happy sigh escaped Kaori.

After a moment, Theo finally pulled back, guiding her to sit on the log with him. "Okay. So there's no guarantee this will work once you're in there. Which makes it that much more dangerous."

"It worked this time. Why wouldn't it work then?" she asked.

He shook his head. "I have no reason to think it won't, but it's possible. If nothing else, planning to sleep at the same time. A number of factors can break that. So we need a plan for times we will both strive to sleep just so if one of us misses one point, we know it's not an entire day before we try again."

She nodded. "Okay. Makes sense."

"And I need you to not take any chances on your own. I want to be prepared when it's time to move." He put her hands between his own. "We are stronger in numbers."

"True," she agreed.

"No matter what, I'm coming in after you if I haven't reached you after two days," he added.

"Wait—"

He stopped her. "No. Anything could happen in there. Including you being killed. I'm not taking any chances that you're tied up and being starved or worse, and if I waited, you die. No. Out of the question."

"Fine. But you have to trust what I tell you when we *do* meet up in our dreams," she stated.

"Of course." He nodded in agreement.

He took her back in his arms and went over a few things for her to watch out for and things he would need her to relay to him. She leaned into his shoulder, listening and adding in her suggestions as well. The sun set over the horizon of the mountains that shaded the backdrop behind the cherry blossom forest that surrounded them.

"So?" Heather's voice betrayed just how eager she was.

Kaori rubbed her eyes. "Huh? What?"

"Did it work?" She practically bounced.

Theo sat up. "Why did you wake us?"

"Because I wanted to know!" She frowned at her brother. "So?" Heather dragged out the word.

Kaori swung her legs off the side of the bed. "Yes. We were discussing a plan before you interrupted."

Heather waved her hand. "You can discuss that while awake. I'm just glad it worked!"

"Hopefully it will again." Theo spoke cautiously.

"It will." Heather clapped, looking at the couple sitting in front of her.

CHAPTER 10

*CW*alking up to the front steps, Kaori wrung her hands. The ornate wood doors loomed in front of her, flanked by landscaped topiaries.

"This is ridiculous, Kaori. You should have just stayed in Japan with your family," she scolded herself.

Three raps on the door, and Kaori took a step back. She crossed her arms over her chest as if there was a chill in the air. But it wasn't the weather that made her cold to the bones. And as she heard someone shuffling on the other side of the door, the chill deepened.

"Hello?" A tall, slender man in a suit greeted her as the door opened.

Kaori gave a slight bow, looking down as she did, then back up. "Kaori Ishida here for Porter Patterson." She offered a smile. "He will know what it is in regard to."

The man took a step aside, opening the door wider. "He is expecting you in the den. Please. After you." He waved an arm for her to enter.

"Of course he is," Kaori replied under her breath as she entered.

Patterson was sitting in an oversized leather chair facing a roaring fireplace, sipping something from a brandy glass. His head twitched slightly when he heard Kaori enter, but he didn't turn. "Come. Sit."

She sighed at the cliché supervillain act he was putting on. "I just want to know that my cousin is safe. And I want to talk about all of these experiments. There's got to be a part of you that *knows* this is wrong."

He didn't reply. Instead, he set his jaw. "I do believe I said to sit."

"This is not a social call, Patterson." She stood her ground.

The man scoffed, his head turning side to side as if she amused him. He placed his hands on the armrests of the chair and lifted himself up. Turning to face Kaori, he looked at her for a long moment, the gaze causing her to grow increasingly more uncomfortable. She felt as if she was under a microscope with how his eyes studied her.

Finally, she broke. "Enough! I want my cousin. And Kai."

The corner of his mouth turned up in an unsettling smirk. "I know what you want. But you see, that's simply not possible. I need her."

"No. You need the life force she and I can provide. We can arrange that. How often does she transfer with you? We can make sure one of us is here to do it. You let us go, release our families and leave us be, and we will keep giving you life. This has gone on long enough! You've had more than the one lifetime you felt you were owed. You've had over a dozen! Enough is enough!"

"Oh Kaori. Sweet, sweet Kaori." He walked forward, closing the gap between them, and placed his hands on her shoulders, leaning in slightly to catch her gaze with his. "But there's so much more I not only need but want."

"You're a—"

He laughed, gripping her shoulders tightly and spinning her around. With a swift movement, he wrapped an arm across the front of her, pulling her in and trapping her against his chest, facing the same way as he was. "Monster? No. That's what your kind is. I'm an opportunist. I'm a product of my own ability to grasp what is before me. Much like this, actually." He turned his head so he could see the side of her face and placed a kiss on her cheek.

He lifted his free hand and motioned to the guard at the door. Kaori watched, searching for Emiko and Kai to come around the corner, ready to try to break free, grab them, and dart out, if there was a chance for it.

Patterson tilted his head back down slightly, his lips grazing her ear. "You see, I've learned a lot through getting to know various people in your family. Not only about your kind but those you love, the world around us, and even myself. And the one thing I know about myself most is that I will do anything to survive at whatever cost."

Kaori heard shuffling from the hallway. Panic rose in her as his words began to fade to the background, her fear of what she was about to see growing.

"I've done a lot to keep this whole thing up, Kaori," he continued. "And I have no intention of stopping. Which is why I am not making the same mistake I did in not taking precautions when I brought you here the first time."

Kaori's vision narrowed as two more large men came into view, but her brain refused to recognize what else she was seeing for a long moment. Finally, things came into view as one man held a limp Heather in his arms and the other struggled to keep his grip on Theo.

Theo roared, a deep, guttural noise.

Patterson waved a finger at him. "Tsk tsk. You don't want to lose your temper so close to the two women you love. Whatever would you do if you hurt one of them?"

Theo's eyes glowed golden; it was a visual struggle for him to not shift. "You take me for some savage animal. Shall we see which of us would win in a fight?"

Patterson wrinkled his nose and chuckled. "You challenge me as if I don't already have the upper hand. Speaking of . . ." He shifted and wrapped his hand around Kaori's throat, tightening just enough to cause her to cough, choking in through a limited airway. "Shall I just snap her neck? I have two of them."

Theo thrashed against the man who held him, and his features began to distort, his nails growing as his facial features started to elongate. And once he started to grow taller, Patterson nodded to the man who held Heather. With a thud, she hit the floor. He was picking up the large, heavy ashtray off the table nearby and swinging it at Theo's head.

Kaori clawed at Patterson's arms. "No!" She tried to escape his grip and get to the unconscious lycan on the floor. She called out, "Theo!"

Patterson started to lose his grip as the small-framed kitsune worked to get to those on the floor. "Ouch!" He let go, reeling back and inspecting a bleeding gash on his hand. "Her, too, David."

And with that, the ashtray was swung again, and Kaori fell to the floor.

~

"Theo? Theo!" Kaori searched the space around her. Then it dawned on her. She wasn't in the waking world any longer. She was in a dream state. Despair hit her as tears started streaming down her face. This wasn't her dreamscape. This was a dense forest with tall, oppressive trees, moss-covered logs, half-dead leaves slowly floating to the ground, skittering wildlife, strange animal noises, a bubbling creek. Nothing like the serene landscape of her Japanese homeland.

Her feet carried her as she stumbled over a fallen log, causing her to ram her shoulder into a nearby tree. She wasn't sure if that was part of her actions there or some sort of forced movement from her waking-world self running into something. But her debate on that came to a halt when she looked down at the log she'd tripped over and saw that it wasn't a piece of wood. It was Theo, unconscious, still, unresponsive on the forest floor.

She ran back over to him, skidding slightly as she dropped to her knees, gripping his shirt.

"Theo! Wake up! Please wake up!" She shook him slightly, but he didn't stir. He was limp against the cold, damp landscape and moss beneath them.

Kaori's heart sank.

She looked around but saw nothing and no one. Closing her eyes, she listened. Nothing came to her except one thing that gave her at least a little comfort—the sound of Theo's beating heart. It was slow and faint but there. Taking comfort in that, Kaori grabbed him by the shoulders and dragged him the short way to the nearest tree. She propped herself up against the bark and cradled his head on her lap, holding his hand with her. "Wake up, Theo. I can't do this without you."

Her eyes scanned the area. She wasn't sure what she was looking for, but every bit of her was on high alert.

Unsure how much time had passed, Kaori jumped when she felt his hand twitch.

"Theo?" She ran her hand over his cheek.

His voice came low, rumbling, deep, and his words incoherent at first. His eyes rolled back, and his lids fluttered.

She sat up more, careful to not jostle him too much. "Are you all right? Theo? Can you hear me?"

"Kaori?" He coughed hard enough to cause him to curl up slightly. His lungs calming a bit, he finally lifted himself up on his elbows. "Where are we?"

She looked around again. "I don't know. I think this is your dreamscape."

"Mine?" He coughed a little more, his hand going to his head. "I didn't know I had one. How did we get here?"

She blinked. "I think it's because you were knocked out first, and the moment they came after me, I reached for you mentally."

He chuckled, a hint of pain in it. "Sounds plausible as this situation will ever get . . . still in awe of this whole dream walking thing." He cringed, his head obviously hurting. "So, wait. They came after you, too? Are you hurt? What did they do?"

She put her fingers to the spot on her head the ashtray had collided with, pulling them away to check for blood. They came off clean, and she wondered if they would in the waking world. "I tried to get to you when they knocked you out."

He nodded, a smirk pulling up one corner of his mouth. "All right then . . ."

His eyes shut, pulling in his eyebrows, betraying his pain.

Kaori scrambled to her knees, leaning over him as she helped him lay back against the tree. "No! Theo, I need you to help. Stay awake. Stay with me. I can't do this on my own."

He swallowed hard and adjusted his sitting position. "I'm here."

"Good." She sat back on her feet. "I mean, I need you to wake up, but I need you to wake up and shift."

"You need what?" He became more alert with her alarming proposal.

"Shift," she stated plainly. "You're stronger in wolf form, both wolf forms. So, shift. I wanted to just break Emiko and Kai out of here, but he's never going to let any of us go, let alone her. It's time we finish my family's nightmare. I've been too soft all these years, too easily persuaded to believe what people wanted me to believe . . . too easily persuaded to see the good in the world around me. But I see now, sometimes there's just evil. Patterson is evil. And if I want any of us to survive this, he has to be taken out of the equation."

"Kill him? I'm not a . . . uh . . ." He stammered over his words.

She scrunched her eyes and shook her head. "I don't mean kill him. You're not a murderer. But if he gets hurt as we get out, then so be it. It's time to stop underestimating him."

Theo sat up and faced her. "I don't want *you* getting hurt, though. We need to consider turning him over to the Court."

She moved to kneel in front of him. Placing one hand on his cheek, she smiled. "Then don't hurt me. I trust you. As far as the Court goes, once we're out of here safely, then the Court can have him. But first we have to get us all out of here." She leaned forward and placed her lips on his.

Theo lay still on the concrete floor. His breathing and heart rate were as slow as they had been in the dreamscape. The noises of people shuffling around him seeped into his consciousness as he began to come around.

"Just put that one in there. She's his sister. We'll find a use for her at some point." Patterson's voice resonated through the room. "Is the kitsune secure?"

"Yes, sir." Another man's voice sounded from across the room.

For a few moments, Theo lay there, assessing how many people were in the room and where. He set his jaw and allowed the shift to start as quiet and still as he could be, trying to give himself a head start before they noticed.

"Shit!" the other man exclaimed. "He's awake."

Footsteps rushed toward Theo, and he sprang up, claws bared and already well into the transformation. The guard who had been holding him in the study was only a few steps away, but it wasn't enough time for the man. As he reached out for Theo, Theo's clawed hand came up, fur-covered and far stronger than his human hand, gripping the man by the throat.

Patterson spun around and saw Theo holding the guard. "Huff and puff, little wolf. Your little girlfriend is tucked away in my brick house."

Theo was deep in his feral state, but he caught a glimpse of Emiko and Kai, each secured in small holding cells across the room, unconscious, and Heather, locked in a cage, lying listless on the floor. Then he saw Kaori. Her arms were strapped to a post on the corner. She, too, was unconscious, slumped against the post. The sight of both of them enraged him. He lunged forward, headed straight for Patterson.

The man brought his fist up, connecting it with Theo's jaw. Theo gripped him by the shoulders and slammed him against the wall behind him. The two clashed for a moment before Patterson lost his grip and slammed back fully.

Theo's clawed fingers dug into Patterson's shoulders, causing him to cry out in pain. "You freak. I have other men in this place. None of you have a prayer of getting out of here alive."

The words washed over Theo in his lycan form. Somewhere deep, they connected with Theo's human brain, but he was more in tune with his savage side that wanted to destroy the man in his grip. This focus faltered only as he heard stirring from where he remembered Kaori sitting unconscious.

The lycan snapped his head to look, seeing her petite form rousing. He was about to turn back to Patterson when something hard collided with the side of his head. Theo stumbled backward a couple steps. It only took a moment before he gathered himself. A low growl welled up from within his chest, and he went for the man, blowing through another slam from the lead pole in Patterson's hand, sending stars through Theo's vision. They scuffled, knocking several items off the nearby table.

～

Kaori's vision was blurry, but she could see them fighting. Unable to move her hands, she realized they were buckled to a post with a set of thick, leather straps. She pulled at them, but they didn't budge. Any thought to shift in order to escape was far from her mind as she stared, frozen with fear at the scene before her.

The two men fell to the floor with Theo on top, pinning Patterson down. A large hand came up and was about to swipe downward, aimed to connect with the side of Patterson's head when the pinned man pulled a syringe out of a fallen wooden box and sunk the needle deep into Theo's side, compressing the plunger fast.

Kaori screamed.

Theo jumped up, the syringe still in his side. Being that he was still in lycan form, his body burned off most of the substance, but he faltered in his footing as some of it rushed through him. His eyes went wide with the understanding that even his heightened metabolism wasn't burning off its full effects.

He looked down at Patterson, who was scrambling on the floor, trying to get up. Then his gaze went to Kaori. Feet awkwardly carrying him over to her, he dropped down, his lycan form slipping away as he slowly started shifting back to his human form. His fingers were clumsy as they wrestled with the straps binding her wrists. Unsuccessful at fully unbinding her, he dropped to the floor.

Kaori called out to him as she worked the straps. "Theo! No!" She was able to finish loosening them enough to free her hands. "What did you give him?" she roared as she stood.

Patterson, out of breath and unable to fully stand, propped himself up against the wall. "A very large dose of what I use to subdue your cousin when she gets out of line. Don't worry there, doll. He's got a system that can take it. He'll have a headache, but he will wake up soon. So let's get you back in those straps. This has gone on long enough."

"I don't think so." Kaori's jaw set.

He laughed. "I just took on a lycan. What do you think you can do to stand up against me?"

"Patterson, this is enough," she warned him.

Another man came rushing into the room at that time, the backup making Porter's face contort into a smirk. "You have no chance against me, let alone against us both."

Her eyes were fixed on him when the other man came at her. The sight of the room around her filled Kaori—Emiko, Kai, and Heather were all locked in cages and Theo was on the floor, unconscious. Patterson was before her, regaining his footing as the other man came closer.

Kaori heard the echo of her mother's voice in her head as they practiced different abilities when Kaori was younger. She wasn't sure it would work, but she raised a hand and allowed it to land on the man's arm as he gripped her. She slowly turned her head and whispered, "Sleep."

To her surprise, with a loud thud, the large man hit the floor.

"What the . . ." Patterson's eyebrows knitted together as he watched his thug go down. And for the first time since she met him, he had fear in his eyes.

She started for him, waving a hand out around her, speaking one word, "Wake." As she did, the others began to stir.

Patterson bent down, shuffling items on the floor around, looking for a weapon. As he gripped a hammer and went to stand, Kaori stepped up to him, placing her hand on his forehead. "You do not deserve this life. You may have been wronged by Tamao, but the exchange you've not only demanded but taken has been far worse."

Patterson's eyes rolled back in his head. His grip on the hammer loosened, and it tumbled to the floor. Lines deepened on his face, and his breath caught.

She continued, not hearing the others coming to around her. "You've caused immeasurable pain. You've taken countless lives. You've done more harm in this world than any amount of good you've done."

A light started to glow around her palm, an essence pulling out from him, swirling around her hand and arm.

"I cannot allow you to continue bringing evil into this world. You must be stopped." She stared into his eyes, which were being drained of their color. "You must be stopped," she repeated.

The lines continued to deepen on Patterson's features. His hair turned white, then a drab gray. And his skin was turning translucent with splotches of darker pigment. His frame become frail.

"Kaori." A hand landed on her arm. Theo's voice penetrated her trance. "You're not a murderer, either."

An inner battle waged in Kaori. Her brows pulled in as her jaw set, her energy pulling harder at Patterson's essence.

"Kaori," Theo pleaded. "You'll have to live with this for the rest of your life."

Her voice cracked as she spoke. "He killed them all. He hurt us beyond repair. He is evil on this earth." A single tear fell down her cheek, her eyes still fixed on the now elderly man in front of her.

Theo wrapped his arms around her. Heather, Kai, and Emiko could be heard as if from a far distance, but she couldn't make out what they were saying. Theo moved into her peripheral vision. "The Court will know what to do with him. They handle supernaturals in this town. It's time to let them choose his fate. Don't take this on your conscience. Trust me."

She blinked a few times, the inner battle still waging, but seeing him, her eyes darted back and forth. The tug on Patterson's essence pulled back some before flickering out. "I . . . I . . ."

Theo ran a hand over her hair. "I know." He kissed her forehead.

The two stood there for a moment before the voices of the others filtered in. Theo held Kaori's shoulders. "Are you all right?"

She looked down at the frail old man on the floor in front of them. "I will be."

Finding a set of keys in Patterson's pockets, Theo refused to speak to him. He simply shook his head before going to each of the cages and opening the doors. Heather embraced her brother for a long moment before joining Emiko and Kai, who were next to Kaori.

They stood over Patterson, looking down on him. He pushed himself up, returning their stare. "What have you done?"

Kaori pursed her lips, her nostrils flaring. "I've ended you."

He looked at his hands and roared. "No!"

Emiko stepped forward, slapping the man across the face. "She might not be able to kill you, but I can, you monster!"

Kai grabbed Emiko by the shoulders. "No. He doesn't deserve that stage in our history. Theo is right. Let the authorities deal with him."

Blood pooled under the thin skin that covered Patterson's cheek, instantly bruising. "It doesn't stop the others from experimenting on those we already have or searching for more of you."

Kaori shook her head. "It's a start."

She closed her eyes, tilting her head up and taking a breath. Her lips parted to say something more, but when her eyes landed on Patterson, she shook her head and abruptly left the room.

Picking up the phone in the parlor, Kaori phoned in the emergency through the operator. Heather helped Emiko and Kai as they secured the unconscious guard and the aged Patterson. Theo made a round through the house, retrieving clothes and making sure there wasn't anyone else being held there.

Finding Kaori in the kitchen, arms folded around herself as she stood at the large picture window that overlooked the grounds, he wrapped his arms around her and pulled her in. "She's free."

Kaori nodded. "It's over."

"Yes." He kissed the top of her head.

"It's over," she repeated.

They stood there with those two words hanging over them.

After a moment, Theo kissed her head once more, a gentle smile playing on his lips. "We're just beginning." He went to the door to let Sheriff Kasun in.

We hope you enjoyed this story in the Legends of Havenwood Falls series featuring a variety of supernatural creatures. The series is a collaborative effort by multiple authors.

Books in the historical Legends of Havenwood Falls series:

Lost in Time by Tish Thawer
Dawn of the Witch Hunters by Morgan Wylie
Redemption's End by Eric R. Asher
Trapped Within a Wish by Brynn Myers
Blood and Damnation by Belinda Boring
Fated Beginnings by E.J. Fechenda
Emeline by Katie M. John
Released From a Curse by Brynn Myers
A Pack of Lies by Kallie Ross
Kiss the Ashes by Desiree Lafawn
Hidden Truths by Colleen Nye
Wrath and Retribution by Belinda Boring
Changing Fate by Char Webster
Rise of the Witch Hunters by Morgan Wylie
The Drowning Bride by Seven Jane

Also try the main Havenwood Falls series; the YA line, Havenwood Falls High; the darker, sexier side of town, Havenwood Falls Sin & Silk; and the local supernatural college, Sun & Moon Academy.

Subscribe to our reader group and receive free stories and more!

ABOUT THE AUTHOR

Colleen Nye started writing as a teen. Through her school days, she won awards for her poetry and short stories, including a Sarah Endres Award for Young Writers. As an adult, she found that her heart is in the art of writing novels. She is the author of The Unattainable Series (*When in Maui, When in Doubt, When in Love*) (*When in Maui* was a B&N best seller in 2013), *Immersion* (an award-winning novel), *The Long Summer, Letters To Cora*, the Manifest Experiment series (*The Pull* is out as of 2018) and more!

She also has taken part in various anthologies and writing projects such as Writing at the Ledges' second, third, and fourth anthologies (*Seasons of Life, Voices from the Ledges*, and *Promptly Speaking*), all five Debut Collective anthologies, and the Lunchtime Anthologies (*Gable Heights*), among others.

When she's not writing, she's working as a freelance book formatter, among other author services, as well as a corporate merchandiser. Colleen is an avid movie collector and online RPGer and loves to dance.

Follow and contact Colleen at:

Facebook - https://www.facebook.com/authorcolleennye

Twitter - @Colleen_Nye - www.Twitter.com/colleen_nye

Instagram - Authorcolleennye - www.Instagram.com/authorcolleennye

ACKNOWLEDGMENTS

The list of people that I would like to thank and acknowledge as having been a part of my journey up to now are included in the acknowledgments and dedications of my other books.

Yet, for this one, I'd also like to include people like Dan, Steve, Jeff, Bob, Scott, Chris, and the many people that helped me learn pen & paper and tabletop games; my old L.A.R.P. gamers. Plus, Malachi, Garrett, Serephia, Edward, Freki, Mary, Craig, Damiyn, Garrix, Sebastian, Ming, Ye-Seul, Mattaku, Kerli, Kym, Tobias, Zane, Trixie, Emi, Dakota, Logan, illy, Joe, Cade, Raymond, Robert, Atreyou, Faust, Arius, Ruin, Ethan, Asryaal, Weaver, Chigan, Fenice, Wulla, Kosho, Sebastian, Freya, Savannah, Amforte, Rhina, Lucious, Hibiki, Aaron, Aker, Finn, the Lindens, and so many others that have made my virtual-world gaming experience educational and entertaining. Not all have stayed around. And some have been lessons learned. Yet some have enriched my life in ways I will always be thankful for and cherish in ways I cannot explain. But all have taught me about virtual worlds and gaming.

And as always, my girls are my rock, my support system, and my cheering squad: the two people I can count on to always tell me what I need to hear when I need to hear it.

AN EXCERPT

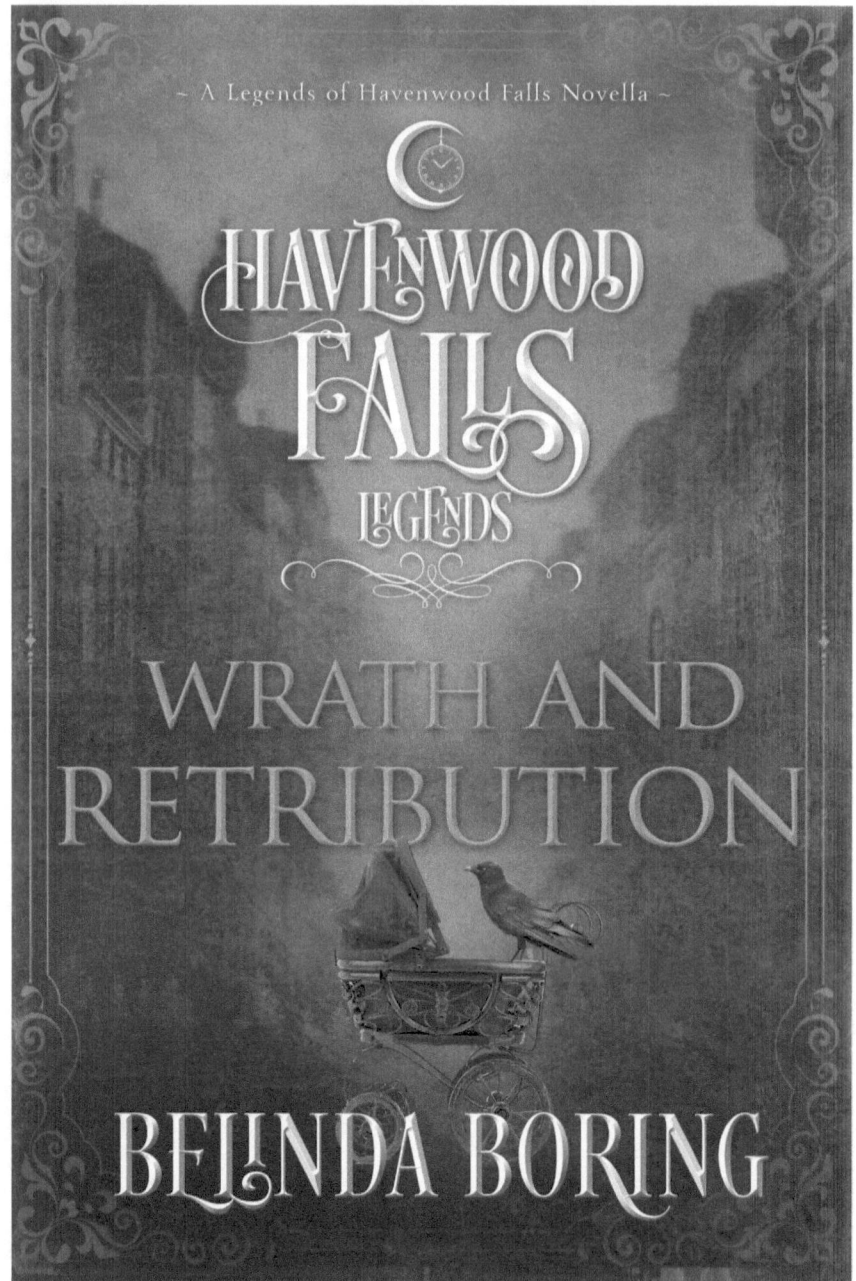

~ A Legends of Havenwood Falls Novella ~

HAVENWOOD FALLS LEGENDS

WRATH AND RETRIBUTION

BELINDA BORING

Wrath and Retribution (A Legends of Havenwood Falls Novella)
by Belinda Boring

In this highly anticipated conclusion to *Blood and Damnation*, cursed vampire Marcus St. James must choose between wrath and retribution—or love.

Following a lead from a seer, Marcus St. James left Victorian England and has landed in Havenwood Falls, still searching for Catriona, the girl who'd managed to break through his fortress and ensnare his heart. He's been searching for her for over a year, since the night she was captured by gypsies and stolen away. But it seems he and his trusted assistant Knox have traveled halfway around the world only to arrive at a dead end.

Cursed to exist as a blood-drinker, Marcus is no stranger to gossip and speculation, so when dead bodies start appearing in Havenwood Falls, he is immediately under suspicion. With two telltale vampire fang marks scarring each body, fear begins to circulate, bringing his own investigation into Catriona's whereabouts to a grinding halt.

But once the dust starts to settle, a new discovery threatens to shatter his world, forcing Marcus to make his most devastating choice yet. Will he forgo his thirst for retribution and abandon justice to keep the peace? Or will his wrath be his undoing and leave him forever cursed?

WRATH AND RETRIBUTION

BY BELINDA BORING

1879 - CATRIONA

The brisk night air felt like a rough slap across my face.

After weeks of endless travel, we'd finally come to what I hoped was the end of our grueling journey. Not that our sudden stop would aid my escape. I was in no condition to flee—to gather up my tattered rags of a skirt and run as though the Devil himself was after me.

Days had stopped making sense in my jumbled thoughts. The months had long since blended into one another, and although I'd valiantly tried to keep track in the beginning, the world was merely a haze of places and strange faces.

There was a small part of me that tried to remain brave and strong. It was from there that a voice whispered to not give up hope, because my husband would find me. Marcus St. James. How the mere thought of him had roused my spirits in the beginning.

Now, a more sinister feeling crept around the edges of my mind—delivering the sober truth that no one was going to rescue me, because I wasn't something he treasured. Should Marcus and Knox indeed find me all the way across the sea, it would be for the sole purpose of satisfying his thirst for vengeance.

No matter how hard I struggled to keep that realization from taking root, the evidence became clearer and clearer as time continued to blur by. He'd once told me I was his property. It was foolish to cling to my heart's hope that he'd grown to care for me.

A brusque female voice broke through my despondent musings. "Is this her?"

I was roughly pulled off the horse, my captor's strong grip wrapped around my arm.

He grunted in response, shoving me hard so I stood within the light's faint halo. "Can you take her?"

My heart skipped a beat. Was this finally the end of the road—an end to the harrowing journey the gypsy had taken me on?

England felt so far away as I slowly looked up and found myself under the intense scrutiny of a dark-haired woman. My gaze quickly darted up and took in my surroundings. Dusk was now upon us, and the night air was filled with the sounds of people heading home for the day. Not this building, however. More light spilled out from the plain glassed windows, seeping out through the lace curtains that hung within.

Piano music unlike any I'd heard before echoed about, matched only by the cheery sounds of chatter and laughter. If I was to wager a guess, my captor had brought me to a saloon or some kind of establishment that catered to drinking and pleasures. We'd stopped at enough along the way for me to recognize the telltale scent of ale and whiskey.

I was definitely a long way from home and the sheltered life I'd been brought up in.

The woman began her slow catlike stalking around me, and suddenly, I felt very, very naked beneath her gaze.

"I have no use for more girls," she tutted as her lips pursed in thought. "Unless you believe she has a talent to please." Without warning, the strange lady grabbed hold of my face, her fingers squeezing my chin until I squirmed in pain. "Do you still have your virtue?"

Part of me wanted to scream . . . wanted to reach out and slap her hard. Once upon a time I would've scratched out her eyes, fought tooth and nail to be free from both of them, but that was then, and this was now. Wisdom was needed—courage—to survive.

I shook my head and looked at my captor, Dimitri. My own personal monster had a name, one he'd boasted in sharing the second he knew we were free from England and his revenge had been successful.

For the briefest of moments, I thought I caught a glimpse of compassion in her eyes. Dimitri was a hulk of a man with a dark piercing stare that caused other men to give him a wide berth. The woman had assumed rightly that he'd taken from my body what he wanted, and that he was far from a gentle lover.

Those were memories I buried deep inside me—far away from the light of day where they wouldn't drive me insane. There were many things I locked away now. The only memory I entertained was Marcus's shout into the night air that he would find me.

I knew that made me a fool, but my stubbornness was the only thing I had left. My pride had been stripped away with each of Dimitri's rough touches.

"She is for my pleasure alone," he responded, slapping me hard on the behind. Gritting my teeth, I forced myself not to cringe or fall to the ground from the force. I still didn't know whether this new woman would become my new jailor or indeed my salvation. I wouldn't show her weakness. I wouldn't show her how completely broken I felt.

"If I take her on, and that is a huge if, Dimitri, I ask that you not manhandle the poor thing." The gypsy male easily towered over her, yet she showed no fear as she pointed her finger, chastising him. Wrapping her arm around my shoulder, she did the unthinkable. For the first time since this whole ordeal begun, someone protected me. "I'll do this because of our family."

And then, as the conversation broke down into a familiar language, my stomach dropped, and my fragile hope was shattered yet again.

Romani.

She wouldn't become my savior or someone I could possibly win over and earn my freedom from. The more I stared at the woman, the easier it was to see the similarities she shared with Dimitri. There was no mistaking that they were kin. The false sense of security that had begun to blossom within me shriveled and died like a neglected rose beneath a cruel sun.

I stared down at the ground and wrapped my arms tightly around myself, hoping to keep the chill from shaking me into pieces. The harder I tried, though, the stronger the quaking became. I was just so tired—exhausted from trying to remain brave. Tears began to flow down my cheeks. They were a luxury I refused to allow myself, but as the sound of their heated conversation broke against me, I lowered my guard and the pain swept in.

Tears for me.

Tears for my future.

Tears for the life that I'd been cruelly ripped from. Never would I complain again about Marcus and his neglect. My heart longed to be back at Smithersby Field—to be standing outside the door to his office where I'd faithfully knocked, hoping to be admitted. I would welcome back that uncertainty a hundred times over if it meant that I could be safe within his home.

"Look, you have made her cry, you oaf," the woman blurted, finally turning her attention back to me. The look of compassion had returned to her face—features I'd only just judged as kind, but now couldn't believe. Even as she gently wiped away my tears with the lace handkerchief she pulled out from the front of her bosom, I steeled my resolve. If she was related to Dimitri, then she couldn't be trusted. She was simply another threat to endure.

Pushing past her, Dimitri grabbed me once more and shook me by the arm.

"You're to stay here until I return." His demand was delivered with enough force not to brook any argument. I already knew that any disobedience would incur his anger.

I nodded quickly and returned my gaze to the floor. Submission pleased him. It always hurt less when I pleased him.

He barked out something else in Romani before swinging his leg up and over his horse. Dimitri was going to leave me here—leave me alone for the first time in a year. Traveling from England, he masqueraded us as a married couple, playing the overly protective husband. There hadn't been more than a few seconds where I wasn't being watched by him, yet now he rode off into the night without a single glance back.

The thought of being here in this strange place alone would've once excited me with all the possibilities for adventures. Now, it sent another round of tremors through my body, weakening my knees to the point I staggered forward and clutched onto my new jailor.

"You are safe for now," the woman whispered as she steadied me back on my feet. She remained quiet until I eventually looked up and found her waiting. Now that Dimitri was gone, I studied her.

Her dark hair was pinned back from her face into a loose bun that had pretty white flowers threaded through the strands. I imagined her the age of my mother, had she survived the pox that had rampaged through our small town when I was still a young child. Her cheeks were reddened, and I couldn't tell if it was from the chilly air kissing her skin or because she was a woman who wore rouge. Unlike mine, her clothing was beautifully stitched, fitting her form perfectly.

"My name is Mrs. Fanny Webster, and this is my home." She gestured back to the building where music still flowed from. That wasn't what confused me, however. She must've been used to people responded to her name because she broke out into laughter. "That is my English name. I adopted a more appropriate one when I arrived in this great country. In my family, what you are called holds certain power, and in the case of the Romani, it often generates fear and hatred."

All I could do was nod in agreement. I'd seen that same emotion consume Marcus—his loathing for gypsies was deep-seated and overshadowed his life. His wrath was at least justified, because of the curse he bore as a result of dealing with them. I'd also seen that same skepticism in the strangers I encountered with Dimitri.

"So," I spoke, my voice soft and scratchy from the lack of use, "you are to be my new owner?"

This earned me another round of laughter, this time louder and heartier than before. "Do you desire that?" She reached to brush aside a strand of hair, and this time I did flinch. I wasn't used to being shown such kindness. "What shall I call you?"

"Catriona," I answered reluctantly.

"Well, Catriona, while you are not free to leave, you are not prisoner here in my home. You will simply stay with me until Dimitri returns." She said it so matter-of-factly, as though the lies that came rolling off her tongue didn't bother her.

"I believe that's the very definition of being owned, Mrs. Webster," I uttered, surprised at my brazenness. I waited, breath held, for the slap that would've followed such a retort to Dimitri, but none came.

"We all have our parts to play," came her response. Hitching up her skirts, she guided me up the back wooden stairs into the building she called her home. One glance inside told me everything I needed to know. This was far from the kind of "home" I was accustomed to, and more like the establishment I'd assumed it to be.

Everywhere I turned were half-dressed women being intimate with gentlemen. Some were leaning in close, engaged in sordid conversations that made them blush. Even more disturbing were the few who had hands up their skirts, their heads tipped back in fake delight.

"He left me here in a whorehouse!" I exclaimed in shock. My eyes grew as wide as saucers. Soon other sounds filled my ears—a different kind of music than the piano. I started to back away to the door, careful not to touch anything.

"Things are not what they seem, child." I expected Mrs. Webster to be offended by my disgust, but instead she looked quite proud. "You'll learn that quickly here."

I shook my head back and forth. I squeaked out loud as I bumped into a very large, extremely jovial man. His arms shot around me, and he bellowed in excitement over catching me.

"A new girl!" the drunk gentleman called out, his fingers splayed across my waist. It didn't matter that I hadn't bathed in weeks and carried the dirt from the road on my clothing. Judging from the way his tongue lolled out of his mouth and how his lecherous lips then pursed into a kiss, he only had one thing on his mind.

Mrs. Webster stepped into action and slapped away his advances while tugging me toward her. "Patience, Mr. Jefferson. This one is not for you."

Before he could pout or argue his case, she called for someone—a young girl in a deep green dress—to bring him something more to drink.

I followed behind her in silence as we crossed through the room and then up the stairs to the second floor. It wasn't until she'd successfully gotten me through a small door at the end of a very long hall that she spoke.

"While you reside here with me, I will protect you, but make no mistake. The life you were once accustomed to is over. The sooner you welcome your new reality, the easier you will adjust." She rattled off a short list of instructions—where I'd be sleeping, the few meager dresses she'd managed to find for me, and eating arrangements, but it all became a blur again as exhaustion took over.

"Will . . ." I couldn't quite finish my most pressing question. All I could do was stare at the door that led back downstairs.

"We'll discuss that in more depth tomorrow. For now, change out of those clothes and get cleaned up. Someone will bring you something to eat shortly, and then I suggest you get some sleep."

"But—"

She shook her head. "Tomorrow."

Mrs. Webster left me standing there alone in the center of the room. As I closed my eyes and took in a deep breath, there was only one thought that anchored me, kept me from floating away.

Find me, Marcus. Find me and bring me home.

MARCUS

1879 – EARLY SUMMER – HAVENWOOD FALLS

I was restless.

After almost a year of traveling over ocean and then land, we'd arrived in the mysterious town whose name Lady Hannah had scribbled across the paper she had delivered. During that time, I'd clung to the message like it was a lifeline that somehow connected me to my Catriona.

That was something that had changed—the way I viewed the young woman I'd once considered a hindrance and nuisance. She was far from that now. She was the only creature I would ever scour the earth for, but as much as I'd kept my hope in finding her alive and strong, the past week had drastically attacked it.

Even now, as I stared at the crumpled piece of parchment, looking down at the memorized words written there, I dreaded having to face reality.

There was a good chance she would remain forever lost.

There was an even more convincing possibility that she hadn't survived the treacherous trip across the seas.

"We'll find her," came the optimistic voice from across the room. "Whether we find her alive or find her grave, we'll discover the truth, Marcus."

So much had changed between me and the young man who had left behind everything to follow me on my most important mission. Once he was simply a means to an end—someone to run my errands and provide me with things I couldn't get for myself.

Phineas Knox was now my brother—blood or not.

Our relationship went beyond his oath to help me break the curse that reduced me to a blood-drinking vampire. He had proven in every way that mattered that he would stand by my side—through thick and thin—and his need for justice ran as deep as my thirst for retribution.

We would find the woman who had secured a place in our hearts. Even if it meant dying in the process.

"The thought of her alone out there with that bastard still makes my blood boil," I answered, letting out a heavy sigh and raking my fingers through my hair. There was no disguising the frustration that had become a permanent part of my voice. Everything irritated me, and because of that, my hunger constantly tugged at me. Knox did his best to help assuage the more beastly parts of my nature, but frankly, it was the least of my worries. "Just give me one minute with the Romani scum and I'll be satisfied."

The sentiment was also a steady topic during our daily

conversations. While Knox wasn't as bloodthirsty in his plans for revenge, I knew that once this journey came to an end, the thief wouldn't be identifiable—even to the closest of his kin.

I finally put down the note. Staring at it always left an angry, bitter taste in my mouth and a tight feeling in my chest. Helplessness wasn't an emotion I tolerated, yet that's exactly what I'd been reduced to, and it rankled.

My fist slammed down hard on the desk. "She has to be here." Knox approached, rolling up his sleeve. I shook my head in strong refusal. "No. It's too soon."

Being new to Havenwood Falls, we still hadn't located a fresh blood source, and Knox had decided that he would be my willing donor until something surfaced. We were both extremely cautious not to draw attention to ourselves, ensuring that nothing prevented our moving freely from town to town.

Catriona was our priority.

My bloodlust had to be managed, but even now I pushed down the hunger that gnawed away inside me.

"Just enough to take the edge off, Marcus." And with that, he shoved his bare wrist in my face. "Quit being a stubborn arse and take what you need." When I continued to refuse, Knox finally grabbed me by the shirt and dragged me in front of the bronze-framed mirror hanging on the wall. Whisper Falls Inn had comfortable enough accommodations, and while it paled in comparison to Smithersby Field, it met our needs. "Unless you'd like to take up Madame Luiza's offer and have her bring bottled blood to you. There's also the den. You decide."

I hated being reliant on anyone. It was bad enough that I needed Knox in order to survive and not reveal my vampiric nature. Despite being told that arrangement could be made for me, I was hesitant to become indebted to this town and the citizens living here.

I stared into the mirror and saw more evidence that I needed to drink.

The reflection staring back at me looked like a man dancing precariously along the edge of mania. My long hair was tousled from my constant pulling at it in annoyance, and the sunken expression around my eyes spoke of the countless nights when sleep had evaded me.

"You look like shit," Knox commented. There was no humor in his tone. He knew exactly how dangerous I was when my thirst was left unchecked. We'd had to flee a few towns along the eastern coast of America because I'd foolishly overestimated my own strength. The last thing I wanted was to leave a trail of dead bodies behind us.

I finally nodded, submitting to his common sense. "We need to find her, Phineas." I repeated my desire again before pressing my lips to the pulse at his wrist. I closed my eyes and pictured her face. "I can't lose her."

My fangs dropped instantly, and with gentle care, I slipped them into his flesh. That first drop of blood hit my tongue like a lightning bolt, zinging power and electricity through my veins. It was the same each and every time I tasted blood. Hunger exploded within my chest, and I fought to keep the temptation to gorge myself in check.

Knox placed his hand at the back of my head when I tried to pull away, resisting the urge to take more. He was another one who often overestimated his limits, making us quite the pair. There was nothing more terrifying than realizing how closely I had brought him to death. I'd made that mistake twice and vowed never to let it happen again.

What I didn't confess out loud was I would've rather drained some stranger in an alley than kill the only man I considered my brother. He was the one who kept me human during this past year.

I wouldn't repay him by being greedy.

My teeth slid back in, and I began my count to ten. Just ten seconds, and that would need to be enough.

There was something intimate between us whenever blood was exchanged. It deepened the love that I had for Knox. It produced a level of gratitude I'd never experienced before.

When I pulled back a second time, he didn't stop me. Instead he simply sat there beside me with his eyes closed, a slight sheen of sweat across his forehead.

"Did I take too much?" I asked, already knowing his response. It was always the same.

He shook his head and raised a shaking hand to his mouth, wiping softly across his lips. A trickle of blood streamed from the two bites at his wrist, and I swiftly took hold of his arm and brushed my tongue across the wounds. Within seconds, any hint of what I'd just done was gone.

"You took what I freely gave, Marcus." I didn't like the quiver in his voice. I hated how weak it made him sound—how weak I'd made him.

"No more, you hear me?" I countered firmly. With each breath I took, I grew stronger as his life force swept through my entire body. I didn't need to peer in the mirror again to know that vibrancy had returned to my features. The guilt that always followed feeding from Knox fueled my need to break this curse.

I didn't want to be the monster anymore.

I didn't want to hurt those I loved.

Knox's eyelids fluttered open, and he gave me a sidelong glance. "This is the safest way, and you know it."

There was a slight hint of red returning to his cheeks, but not enough to stem my worry.

"No more," I repeated. Leaving him to sit by himself, I gathered up a plate of leftovers from last night's meal and brought it to him. "I won't risk you again, Knox, and that's the end of it. Look me in the eyes and tell me that it's not taking a toll on you."

He took the plate from me and slowly broke off a piece of stale bread. Knox took a bite before tossing it back with the rest of his meal. "At least let me find an alternative, Marcus. Please. I need to find more ingredients for your daily elixir as well. Perhaps Havenwood Falls has something available for people like us."

That had definitely been a surprise. Not only had Lady Hannah's message led us far from home, but it had brought us to a small, newly established town where supernatural creatures like me lived amongst humans. From what we'd been able to discover, they lived in relative peace, following the rules that the governing council enforced.

"Don't you think Saundra Beaumont would've told us that when we met with her?" I answered, going over that brief meeting in my mind.

While a man called Roman Bishop had met us and led us into

town a week ago, it was a young witch who had approached us the next day and provided an introduction and small tour. There weren't many instructions other than the obvious—don't stand out and don't cause trouble. We in turn shared our intentions and what had brought us to Havenwood Falls. Miss Beaumont had patiently listened to our ordeal and offered some suggestions about searching for Catriona. She was especially intrigued—and seemed none too pleased—that a seer all the way in London had revealed the existence of her secret town.

When we parted ways, it was with the promise that she would ask her own questions and perhaps shed more light on my wife's whereabouts. As a witch, she had access to a coven, and no amount of begging and bribery from me could convince her to allow me to be there when she did.

"Things are done differently here," she'd added before excusing herself.

It wasn't until Knox had convinced me that we needed to play by the rules and not storm the keep, so to speak, that I calmed down and accepted that there were things beyond my control.

I would be nice and polite.

I would nod and smile, if needed.

But my patience was wearing thin.

I needed something—anything—some kind of news to hold on to.

Jumping up, I paced back and forth before striding over to the window to peer out. It was still somewhat early in the morning, and the streets were only now starting to get busy. All I could think of was that someone out there held the information I desperately needed. "Eat more and then go run your errands. I need time to think."

"I'd prefer we go out together," came his reply. Knox sounded stronger, and sure enough, his skin had returned to its usual color. A few more meals beneath his belt and he'd be back to normal.

"I don't need babysitting. Contrary to your false assumptions, I am quite capable of looking after myself." My response came out harsher than I intended. The room fell silent as I felt him measure my words. "Knox," I added curtly, "I won't be coddled."

I saw the exact moment when he relented. With a brisk nod, his gaze returned to his plate as he polished off the remaining food.

"Be careful," Knox answered after swallowing the last mouthful of his meal.

Peeking through the curtains again, I gazed up at the sky. It was another bright, sunny summer day, and my eyes trailed up to where the mountain peaks stood tall and proud. "Perhaps we should go exploring. The gypsy may have her camping out there in the wilderness somewhere. That may be why we haven't found her here in town."

"I'll gather provisions, then."

Suddenly I needed to be out in the fresh air, and not breathing in the staleness of the room. "Good."

With a quick farewell, I closed the door behind me and made my way toward the stairs leading down. In my haste to get out, I bumped into the small human woman responsible for cleaning the rooms.

"Sorry, sir," she exclaimed, ducking her head apologetically. "I didn't see you there."

Steadying her, I offered a smile that said no harm was done. It triggered a thought. "Do you mind if I ask you a question?"

Her stricken expression turned into one that was willing to help. "Of course." Her blue eyes brimmed with eagerness. "How can I assist?"

"If I wanted to find something here in town but I didn't know who best to ask, where would you suggest I go?" When her brow furrowed in concentration, I added more to clarify what I needed. "Is there someone I could talk to that knows things about the town?"

That appeared to make things much easier, as she nodded excitedly. Looking to see if anyone else was nearby, she leaned in and whispered like we were joint conspirators. "I'm not supposed to know what goes on in there, but everyone does, and it's not really a secret. Just don't tell anyone who told you, because I would get a thrashing from my father. Respectable folks don't go there."

Her response intrigued me. "This will be between you and me. You have my word as a gentleman."

That elicited a giggle from her.

"You need to talk to Mrs. Fanny Webster." She said it as if the name should spark some kind of recognition. I'd never heard it before, and my face must've reflected that, because in an even softer whisper the young maid continued. "She runs the whorehouse here in town."

It was my turn to laugh.

Of course. If there was one truth that was universal in this world, it was that loose morals led to looser lips, and many a secret was spilled in such establishments where liquor flowed freely and legs were spread for money.

"Mrs. Fanny Webster," I repeated, making sure I understood her perfectly. I had. "You have done me a great service this morning, Miss." Kissing the back of her hand like she was one of England's finest ladies in the peerage, I bowed deeply and continued on my way.

I was about to visit my first whorehouse.

Perhaps this journey hadn't led to a dead end after all.

Purchase *Wrath and Retribution* where books are sold.